CONTAMINATION

BOOK FOUR: ESCAPE

BY T. W. PIPERBROOK

ABOUT CONTAMINATION 4: ESCAPE

Dan and Quinn Lowery may have survived the initial infection, but their journey is far from over.

Their once-safe location has now been compromised, overrun by the agents and the infected.

Now, in order to survive, they must first escape...

AVAILABLE NOW!
CONTAMINATION PREQUEL
CONTAMINATION 1: THE ONSET
CONTAMINATION 2: CROSSROADS
CONTAMINATION 3: WASTELAND
CONTAMINATION 4: ESCAPE
CONTAMINATION 5: SURVIVAL
CONTAMINATION 6: SANCTUARY

Want to know when the next book is coming out?
Sign up for NEW RELEASE ALERTS
and get a FREE STORY!
http://eepurl.com/qy_SH

PART ONE
FULL COLLAPSE

"DADDY, WAKE UP!"

Hands pawed frantically at Dan Lowery's arm, and a voice hissed in his ear. When he opened his eyes, he could just make out the frightened visage of his daughter, her eyes wide, lips trembling. He immediately grabbed for the 9mm he had tucked under his pillow and jolted from the floor.

"What is it?" he mouthed.

His daughter pointed to the side window of the RV, where a thin sliver of moonlight crept through a crack in the blinds. He padded over to it and peered out, prepared to see a face on the other side, fingernails rapping on the glass.

The window was empty.

Still, he knew his daughter had heard or seen something. She wouldn't have woken him up if she hadn't.

He pressed his forehead against the pane. They'd positioned the RV diagonally in a corner of the lot, allowing them a view of the entire salvage yard as well as a clear path to the front gate. At the slightest hint of trouble, Dan wanted to be ready to leave.

Now, as he stared out at the dark and ominous lot, he wondered if the time had come.

Between the absence of power and the darkness of the night, the salvage yard was a tangle of shapes and shadows, and if he stared hard enough, almost all of them appeared suspicious. Ever since they'd arrived, Dan had felt less than comfortable, but given their situation, the options were limited.

It didn't help that they were alone on the property.

Quinn joined him at the window and gripped his shoulder. With her free hand, she pointed to a group of dark objects in the yard. Dan followed her stare and felt his body tense up.

One of the shadows was moving.

"Stay still," he whispered.

The figure was hovering by one of the junked vehicles near the front entrance. Every so often, its head would swivel or its arm would wag.

Dan scoured the rest of the salvage yard, but saw no indication that there were other intruders. So far they'd been lucky. In the few days since their companions had left, Dan and Quinn had seen only a few straggling creatures make their way into the salvage yard, and each time he'd easily taken care of them through the fence. None had posed any immediate threat to him or his daughter.

Of course, none had found their way inside until now.

Dan stared at the creature lurking in the shadows, unnerved. He'd assumed that if one of the things attempted to climb the fence, he'd hear it, asleep or not.

This one seemed to have simply appeared.

No matter how it had gotten in, Dan knew he had to take care of it. He wouldn't rest until he did.

He rose to his feet. Before he could turn, his daughter snagged his attention.

"Dad, look!" she whispered.

Two more shadows had appeared next to the other one. Unlike the first, these were moving quicker, and it looked like they were headed in the direction of the RV. He scoured the yard.

What he saw next made his heart drop in his chest.

The front gate—the one that he'd kept locked since they'd arrived—was hanging open.

Dan lowered the shade.

"What're we going to do, Dad?" Quinn asked.

"We're leaving."

"But Dad—"

"Listen to me carefully, honey. I need you to get in the passenger's seat and buckle your seatbelt, just like we talked about earlier. Can you do that?"

Even in the darkness, he could see the outline of her head as she nodded. He stalked toward the front of the vehicle. His daughter followed, clinging to the back of his shirt.

He'd just reached the driver's seat when something clicked the door handle. He froze, reached for his daughter. A similar noise sounded from the opposite side of the RV.

Thank God he'd locked the doors.

Pistol in hand, he crept to the driver's seat and peered out the window. At the same time, a shadow scurried to the rear of the vehicle. He pushed his daughter toward the passenger's seat and sat down himself.

Earlier, he'd left the key in the ignition. He reached down to verify that it was still there.

It was. He swallowed.

Each day he'd been starting the RV to ensure everything worked, and each day it had fired up without issue.

Here goes nothing.

He turned the key, preparing for the engine to start and expose their position.

Only this time, when he turned the key, nothing happened.

"You've got to be kidding me," he muttered.

He tried again, but to no avail.

"Daddy, what's wrong?" Quinn hissed.

Before he could answer, Dan heard a bang on the rear windows, then the sound of someone trying the door handle in back.

Dammit.

He leapt up from the driver's seat and grabbed his daughter's arm, leading her to the rear of the vehicle. Past their bedding and belongings was a door leading to the bathroom. He found the handle, ripped open the door, and ushered her inside.

"In here," he said.

"But Dad—"

"No arguments, Quinn. Don't come out until I come get you."

"But what if something happens to you? What if—"

"Everything will be fine, honey."

He gave her one last squeeze and then shut the door. In spite of his words, he was far from convinced. The banging had increased in fervor; it sounded like the doors were going to crash open.

He aimed his pistol in all directions, trying to anticipate which one of them would fly inwards first.

What he didn't anticipate was the front windshield shattering.

Glass spattered all around him and bullets whisked through the interior of the RV. Dan dove to the ground. He hit the floor hard, scraping his elbows and knees on the thin carpet, and bit the inside of his lip. Blood sprayed the inside of his mouth, and he covered his head as glass rained down on top of him.

He heard shouting and commotion from outside now, and he struggled to his knees, certain someone would be coming in after them.

At that point, they'd be trapped.

Dan crawled to the front of the vehicle and hid

behind the driver's seat, clutching his pistol to his chest. The gunfire had ceased. He poked his head around the headrest, trying to get a glimpse of the outside.

The second he peered out, a pair of headlights snapped on from the salvage yard and illuminated the interior of the RV. He slipped out of sight, but he was too late. The voices grew louder; he'd been seen.

Who was out there? Was it the agents? A gang? Another band of survivors?

Regardless of who it was, one thing was for certain: if Dan and Quinn remained inside the RV, they were sitting ducks.

He looked back at the bathroom. The door had opened to a crack, and his daughter's face had emerged from the darkness. She was calling out his name.

Dan motioned for her join him. She scampered across the floor and into his arms, squeezing him tight. He handed her the pistol.

"Remember what I showed you?"

She nodded. He pointed to the safety.

"Just like we talked about."

Yesterday he'd given her some simple instructions on using the weapon, telling her that someday she might need to use it.

He just hadn't expected that day to come so soon.

She held the gun, eyes wide. While she stared

at the weapon, Dan reached underneath the bench seat next to them and pulled out a shotgun.

"Stay behind me," he whispered. "We'll go out the side door."

He pointed to the passenger's door across from them. For the moment, all was quiet.

He crawled over to it, unlocked the door, and grabbed the handle. He looked back at his daughter and put his finger to his lips.

"On three," he mouthed.

He counted silently with his fingers, then threw it open. Instead of flying ajar, the door stopped with a *thud*, knocking into someone on the other side.

A man in a white coat was waiting for them.

Dan let loose with the shotgun. The impact of the blast flung the agent backwards, riddling his coat with blood, and he collapsed into the dirt.

The yelling rose to a fever pitch.

"Come on, Quinn!" Dan shouted.

The two of them jumped into the dirt. Dan hung behind the open door, then sidestepped into the open and took an officer's stance. He fired off another round toward the gate. A sickening grunt sounded in the distance.

"Let's go!"

A broken-down Camaro was parked about twenty feet away. He guided his daughter toward it, and they ducked for cover. Gunfire exploded once again. He looked down at the shotgun, realizing he'd expended the last two rounds.

How many of the agents were there?

A few days earlier, two of the agents had paid a visit to the salvage yard, and Bubba, the salvage yard owner, had killed them. Afterwards, the survivors had driven the agent vehicles out into the desert to hide them.

Despite taking care of the men, Dan had suspected that the other agents might not be far behind. He just wished he and his daughter had left sooner.

He glanced next to him, taking in his daughter's small frame under the glow of the headlights that cut across the yard. She was still clinging on to the pistol, her hands shaking.

I've got to get us out of this.

In just a few days, the two of them had survived hordes of the infected, car chases, and encounters with the agents. On top of that, they'd somehow managed to keep their sanity in spite of losing Julie — Dan's wife, and mother to Quinn.

And here they were again, fighting for their lives. It didn't seem fair.

Dan reached over and borrowed the pistol from his daughter and aimed it over the back of the Camaro. From their new position, he had full view of the attacker's vehicle — a cargo van with the lights blazing, parked just inside the front gate.

Two agents were lurking beside it. When they spotted Dan, they lifted their weapons and started to advance.

Dan fired off several rounds of suppressive fire, forcing the men back to the van. One of them opened the driver's side door and fired around it, and Dan hunkered down, listening to bullets rip through the air. Quinn lay on the ground next to him, her hands clamped over her ears.

Bullets dinged off the side of the Camaro.

After a few seconds the shooting stopped. Dan poked up again and squeezed off a round. This time he hit his mark, and the agent to the left of the van fell to the ground. The other man — hiding behind the driver's side door — appeared to be reloading.

Instead of crouching again, Dan remained poised and ready, and when the other man reared his head, he aimed and fired.

The bullet struck the last man in the chest, sending him sprawling to the ground.

Two for two.

Dan exhaled the breath he'd been holding.

He waited several more minutes, certain that someone else would emerge, but the yard remained silent, and there was no one else in sight. The air was thick with dust and dirt, creating a smoky residue under the headlight's glare.

The men on the ground stayed motionless.

Even if he'd gotten all of them, he was certain there'd be more coming. There was no question what needed to occur next: he and his daughter needed to leave.

Dan wiped a bead of sweat from his forehead

and turned to face Quinn. Hopefully she hadn't been watching. She'd already seen enough bloodshed; the last thing he wanted to do was expose her to any more.

To his surprise, the ground next to him was empty.

Where was she?

He swiveled to find her, heart thumping, scanning the perimeter of the yard. Why did she leave his side? She'd been right next to him a second ago; he couldn't imagine her running off without him.

What had happened?

"Quinn!" he shouted, panic overtaking him.

He looked in all directions. Even if he had to search the whole yard, the whole *state*, he'd find her. He glanced back to the RV, thinking that maybe she may have run there. He'd only taken two steps when he heard a noise to his left. He turned and saw a four-foot shape in the dark.

Quinn.

He opened his mouth to speak, but before he could call her name, a dark shadow appeared from behind her. Dan's entire body tensed.

Walking toward him, gun pressed against his daughter's temple, was another one of the agents.

2

"I F YOU HARM HER IN any way, I swear to God—"

Dan let his voice trail off, realizing that his words were having little effect on the man. The agent's eyes were cold and dark, beyond reason. The question wasn't whether he would pull the trigger, but *when*.

Dan dropped the pistol and threw his hands in the air. If he were to have any chance at overtaking the man, he'd have to comply. Hopefully he'd buy himself a few more seconds; a little more time to think.

"Please let her go," he said. "She has nothing to do with this."

The agent inched forward, smiling now. He didn't speak a word; instead, he tightened his arm around the girl's throat. Quinn was crying soundlessly, arms at her sides. The look in her eyes made Dan feel helpless and enraged.

His daughter was all he had left, and he'd failed her.

He stared at the man's expression, hoping for a sign of something—*anything*—that he could use to free his daughter. But there was nothing. Any trace of emotion or compassion was gone.

It was then that he saw two shadows—one coming up on the agent's right, the other on the agent's left.

Dan's hopes sank further. Not only was this man alive, but it appeared there were others as well. He bristled, knowing that he'd have no choice but to take action, that he and his daughter might be killed in the process.

It wasn't until the shadows came into the light that he realized that the figures weren't agents at all, but two of the creatures.

Sensing Dan's switch in attention, the agent turned his head to the side, catching a glimpse of the two things coming up behind him. His grin quickly faded. The creatures hissed and spit, and within seconds, they were on top of him.

The agent let go of his hostage and began to fire at the advancing infected. He took them out quickly, aiming at their heads.

While the agent was distracted, Dan had taken the opportunity to dive for his own weapon. Before the other man could spin back around, Dan pumped out three bullets, striking the agent in the back. The man collapsed facedown into the dirt.

Dan leapt toward his daughter and squeezed her tight. He looked over her shoulder at the man he'd just shot. The agent lay motionless, a pool of blood blossoming on his back.

He shuddered.

In his old life, back when he was a police officer, shooting a man from behind would've been illegal. Now he'd done it without a second thought.

Regardless of his methods, Dan had been able to protect himself and his daughter, and that was what counted.

All the rules and laws he'd followed as a police officer were gone; the only thing left was to survive.

"Where are we going now, Daddy?"

Dan stared at his daughter, then at the pile of their belongings on the ground. In this new world of uncertainty they'd been reduced to a few blankets and pillows, and neither had changed or bathed in a week. Their meals had consisted of canned and labeled food, and sleep, when it came, was fitful.

And now they were going to be upheaved again.

Dan gathered their things and tossed them in the back of the Subaru Outback. Before Bubba had died, he'd helped to replace the shattered rear windshield, and Dan had cleaned the glass from the backseat. He'd contemplated taking one of the RV's, but given the size and lack of maneuverability, he decided to stick with his wife's station wagon.

At least they'd have the stability of the family vehicle.

"Wait here, honey," he said, once his daughter had gotten inside.

He closed the door and locked the car. He'd since covered up the bodies on the ground, hoping to at least spare her from having to look at them repeatedly, but he still needed to move the cargo van away from the front entrance.

Morning was fast approaching, and daylight was working its way through the cracks and crevices of the nearby mountains. Dan walked across the dusted grounds, surveying the carcasses of automobiles, reliving the memories they'd made there.

Since the other survivors had departed, the salvage yard had felt empty, and he'd found himself thinking of them daily. Had Noah made it home to Portland to find his family? Had Sam and Delta found what they were looking for in Salt Lake City?

A part of him was afraid that one of them might return, in trouble and in need of assistance, and find the yard abandoned. At the same time, Dan had a duty to protect his daughter, and he knew it was no longer safe here.

Just in case, he'd left a note in the guard shack.

The lights of the cargo van were still on, playing over the empty lot. He used the glow to search the rest of the yard. Aside from the three agents and the several creatures they'd killed, there was nothing more of concern.

After one last precautionary sweep of the

van, he leapt into the driver's seat. The key was still inside. He fired up the engine and drove the vehicle through the gate, parking it next to a row of RV's.

He was about to shut off the van when a radio cackled on the dash.

Dan froze.

"Sanchez, you there?"

He stared at the receiver, but kept his hands on the steering wheel. Did the other agents know what had happened? Were they waiting for a report?

The voice rang out again.

"We need all agents back at the compound. There's been a breach."

Dan let go of the steering wheel, his mind brimming with questions. Who'd breached the compound? Was it the government?

He reached across the console, ready to engage the person, and then thought better of it. Any contact with the agents could jeopardize his and his daughter's safety. There could be others nearby, and if they sensed trouble, they might follow their companions to the salvage yard.

He thought of Sam and Delta, and for a fleeting second, he pictured that maybe *they* had been the breach, that somehow they'd found their way inside.

But that would be impossible, wouldn't it?

Dan waited another minute, but the man on the other end did not return. In any case, it was time to get moving. Sooner or later, the agents would figure out that these men had been killed, and they'd send others looking for them.

Hopefully by that time Dan and Quinn would be long gone.

He killed the engine and departed the vehicle. He could see Quinn watching him from the passenger's seat of the station wagon, and he gave her a smile and a wave.

Although they were leaving, he had no clue as to their destination. He just hoped that by abandoning the salvage yard, they weren't trading one threat for another. In the salvage yard, at least they had the gates to protect them. On the roads, they'd be reduced to the doors and windows of the vehicle.

Dan circled to the back of the station wagon, peering in for one last check of the contents. He'd stored the remainder of their packaged food there, along with some additional reserves he'd found in the agent's van. He'd also packed several weapons: two pistols, the empty shotgun, and several bats and crowbars, along with a few containers of gasoline.

Given what they were up against, it was hardly enough to feel safe, but it was the best he could do.

With the cargo secure, he motioned for Quinn to unlock the doors and then got inside to join her. He noticed she was holding a teddy bear in her hands, and he wrinkled his brow.

"Where'd you get that?"

"I found it in the guard's shack the other day," she said.

The bear, which at one time might have been white, had taken on a brown tinge, the fabric of its blue pants faded with age.

"What's his name?" Dan asked.

His daughter smiled. "Samson."

"Is Samson ready to go?"

"Yup."

"All right, you two; hold on tight."

Dan forced a smile, then switched the car into drive and rolled forward. A minute later he was navigating through the open gates.

Night had officially passed the torch to day, and the heat came down in waves over the desert. For safety reasons, Dan had instructed his daughter to keep the windows up, choosing instead to run the air conditioner at its lowest setting.

It was barely enough to keep them cool, and not enough to stop them from sweating. He padded his forehead with his sleeve, watching as his daughter did the same.

"Can I roll my window down a crack, Daddy?" his daughter implored.

He sighed, taking in the empty roads around them.

"OK, but be ready to roll it up if we see something."

She nodded and fiddled with the window controls, lowering the window about halfway. Dan shut off the air conditioning. Given their limited resources, he'd need to conserve as much fuel as possible.

After a few more minutes of silent play with the teddy bear, his daughter turned on the radio. She scrolled the dial from left to right, finding nothing but static.

"Do you think anybody's still out there?" she asked.

"I'm sure there are people out there just like us."

"Will we see any of them?"

"I bet we will, honey. We'll just have to be real careful about who we talk to and who we trust."

His daughter stared out the window at the wide expanse of desert. At the moment the road was long and straight; there were no signs of civilization in sight. However, Dan knew that was soon to change. In a matter of minutes he'd need to choose a direction.

He just had no idea what that direction might be.

He was still contemplating that question when Quinn piped up next to him.

"Do you think Aunt Meredith's OK?"

Dan sighed. It'd been years since they'd spoke to Julie's sister. Meredith lived in Settler's

Creek, Oklahoma. Due to the distance between St. Matthews and Settler's Creek, they'd lost contact.

"I bet she's fine," he said.

"Can we go visit her?"

Dan paused. Julie's sister had never been fond of Dan, claiming that he'd forced Julie to move away from her hometown. Three years ago, the two sisters had gotten into a heated argument, and neither had spoken since.

Dan had always thought that Julie should patch things up, but the more time that passed, the less likely that had seemed.

He wondered what Meredith was doing now, and if she'd heard of what had happened. Was the same thing happening in Oklahoma that was happening here? Did she have any idea that her sister was dead?

He swallowed the lump in his throat, realizing that he owed Quinn an answer.

"I'm not sure if that would be a good idea."

"Why not?"

"Settler's Creek is hours away. That'd be a long, dangerous drive."

"What if things are safe there?"

Dan paused, reconsidering.

Quinn had a point. Regardless of the distance, his daughter's safety was paramount. If Meredith had a safe place to keep them, it might be worth the trip.

Dan pictured the farm that Julie and Meredith had grown up on. For years their parents had procured their own food, relying on income from their crops to support themselves.

When Julie's parents had died, Meredith had taken over the farm, intent on keeping up the family tradition. It was a noble cause, but one she'd ended up taking on alone.

Early on, Julie had voiced her desire to sell it, but Meredith had disagreed, opting to live on it instead. The farm had always been a source of contention between them, and Julie's marriage to Dan had only made things worse.

In hindsight, the arguments they'd had seemed small, insignificant.

Dan regretted they had ever happened.

"That might actually be a good idea, Quinn," he said finally.

His daughter beamed.

"There's a chance that the virus hasn't hit there yet, and even if it has, the crops on the farm should be untouched. Come to think of it, finding Aunt Meredith may be our best bet."

"Do you think she still has Ernie?"

Ernie was Meredith's miniature poodle, a spunky black dog that loved to jump on unsuspecting visitors. Meredith had gotten the dog around the time that Quinn was born.

"I bet Ernie's still there," Dan said. "But he might be a little older than you remember."

His daughter smiled at the news, suddenly filled with a burst of energy. She held up the teddy bear.

"Did you hear that, Samson? We're going to see Aunt Meredith and Ernie!"

Dan smiled back, glad that they'd made a decision. In spite of that, he kept his relief contained. Making the decision was easy.

Getting there would be the hard part.

3

EREDITH TILLY HAD BEEN RUNNING the television set for a week straight. Most of the stations had gone down, and of the reports she received, most were speculation. Although few details were known, one thing was certain.

No one had been inside the contamination zone for long and survived.

She walked from her couch to the window, peering out over the field of crops outside. Aside from a few circling crows, there wasn't a creature or a human in sight. Thank God she lived in a rural area.

It was days like these that made her glad she'd kept her parent's farm.

At the same time, she felt a deep sense of loneliness and isolation. She hadn't had a visitor in days, and even before that, her chats with the neighbors had been short and anxious.

Nobody knew what was happening, or what was coming next.

Reports of the contamination had started in Arizona and New Mexico, but in the days following, there had been rumors that it had spread into Oklahoma. Meredith had yet to see any evidence of it herself, but then again, she wasn't exactly living in the city.

Her daily routine consisted of interacting with more animals than people, and that wasn't saying much.

Despite the fact that she'd been safe thus far, she was wracked with worry. Ever since the initial reports had come in, she'd been thinking of her sister.

She'd been calling her every day.

All attempts at communication to the affected areas had been useless. The phones in the contamination zone were down, and according to the news, even people at the edges of the state had long since lost contact.

Meredith's biggest fear, even greater than her own safety, was that she would never speak to Julie or her family again.

Three years ago she'd gotten into an argument with Julie over the farm, and they hadn't spoken since. Although Meredith regretted the fight, she'd been stubborn, refusing to make the first move to patch things up.

Now, she'd do anything to make things better. She just hoped she wasn't too late.

A few days prior she'd taken her car into town, ready to drive to Arizona herself if necessary. But according to the townsfolk she'd run into, the government had blocked the roads and highways; any attempts to get through had been prohibited.

She'd even heard rumors of people being shot.

Although she couldn't see how that could be true, she'd resolved to wait a few more days, hoping to receive word from her sister. Surely the outbreak would come to an end.

Something had to give. Things couldn't stay like this forever.

Could they?

She sighed at the window. Regardless of everything she'd heard, she was hopeful that her sibling would contact her soon. She wiped under her eyes, fighting back tears, and let her hand fall to her side.

Almost immediately, something wet hit her fingertips.

She smiled and looked down at the little dog at her feet. "Hi, Ernie!"

The animal was licking her hand, and when she said his name, the dog dove at her mid-section. Meredith reached down and scooped him up, caressing the small patch of fur on his head. The dog snorted in appreciation.

"You're a good boy," she told him.

Outside, the sun had propped itself high in the sky, shining its rays of luminescence onto the crops below. In a few minutes she'd go out and tend them. Tragedy or not, she needed to keep producing, especially if she wanted to eat.

It was July, and the farm was teeming with vegetables: cucumbers, corn, tomatoes, and eggplant. On a normal day she'd harvest the food and bring it into town to sell at the family food stand. Now she'd been keeping close to home, surviving off the food she'd grown.

She no longer trusted anything else.

Meredith set the dog on the floor, ignoring his repeated requests for attention, and resolved to go upstairs and get changed.

Before she had a chance, she heard a shrill, high-pitched noise from the kitchen, and her heart jumped in her chest.

Her phone was ringing.

Who could that be?

Once a day she'd been trading calls with her neighbors, Sheila Guthright—an elderly woman who owned a property to the north, and Ben and Marcy Sanders, a middle-aged couple that owned the property next door. Even though they were all neighbors, their houses were spread far apart: each owned about ten acres of land.

But she'd already spoken to all of them today.

Maybe it's news about Julie.

By the time Meredith got to the kitchen, she was out of breath. Ernie circled her heels. She looked down at him, and he barked, as if he sensed her nervousness.

"Quiet, boy," she said to the dog. She picked up the phone. "Hello?"

"M-Meredith?"

The voice on the other end was cracked and distorted, and she pressed the phone tight to her head, doing her best to hear it.

"Sheila? That you?"

"Yes. Something's wrong with Ben."

"What do you mean? Is he there?"

"Yes."

"Is Marcy with him?"

"No, dear, she's not. And he's acting strange. I told him I'm not going to open the door."

"Does he look sick?"

"He doesn't look well."

"Oh God. Listen, Sheila—"

"He keeps banging, and he won't stop."

"Whatever you do, don't let him in! He might be infected, Sheila!"

Before Meredith could protest further, the phone disconnected. She tapped the lever and frantically dialed back the woman's number, but there was no answer.

She called back a second time, a third. The phone rang and rang.

In a panic now, Meredith hung up and raced for the door.

It was possible that Sheila had been overreacting; that Ben had simply come to visit her. After all, the woman was almost ninety-years-old, and she'd suffered a few bouts of confusion in the past few months. But even still, Meredith couldn't shake the nagging feeling that the woman was in trouble.

She just hoped to God she was wrong.

Meredith flew from the house and into her pickup truck, the keys jangling in her hand. She threw them in the ignition and fired up the vehicle.

The quickest way to Sheila Guthright's house was to take the road. Even though they were technically neighbors, their properties were enormous—it would take Meredith almost ten minutes by foot.

The way it sounded, ten minutes might be too late.

She backed down the fifty-foot driveway to the road, the truck tires crunching gravel, and swerved out onto the pavement. She'd just started driving when she had a sudden thought.

She had no weapons on her.

She glanced back at the property, contemplating going back, but dismissed the idea. She'd already lost enough time as it was, and Sheila needed her help.

From the little footage that the news had been able to gather—footage that had been looped over and over—she knew that things were looking grim. Still, she couldn't imagine it happening here: not in Settler's Creek, and certainly not to people she knew.

Her best bet now was to hightail it to Sheila's house. In the event something was happening, she'd figure it out when she got there. Chances are that Ben had run into some medical emergency; maybe his wife was sick and needed help.

Sheila must've gotten it all wrong.

Meredith continued to convince herself of these things as she drove the rural road to the woman's house. In just a few minutes, she'd driven by the wooden fence that marked the edge of her property. In a few more she'd hit the driveway leading to Sheila's house.

She turned in faster than she should and gunned the accelerator. Sheila's driveway was as long as Meredith's, about fifty feet or so, and she could already make out Sheila's Buick Regal parked at the top.

To her surprise, there was no sign of Ben's pickup truck.

Ben and Marcy lived on the other side of the property, to the south, and were also a considerable distance away. Unless Ben was looking for exercise, he normally would've driven, especially if there was an emergency.

Meredith swallowed the lump in her throat. She climbed the remainder of the driveway in her pickup, and when she'd reached the top, she killed the engine and stared at the house.

Sheila lived in a modest white Victorian, with a railed front porch and several front steps leading up to it. The house contained two floors, an upstairs and a downstairs. Meredith was consistently surprised that the ninety-year-old woman was able to navigate her way between both.

Almost all of the shades of the house were

open. That made sense, because Sheila was an early riser.

What didn't make sense was that the front door was open as well.

Meredith leapt from the truck and walked the yard, then peered inside from the foot of the porch stairs. Inside, she could see the staircase leading to the second floor and segments of the living room and kitchen.

In none of those places did she see Sheila or Ben.

The house was silent, vacant, as if the occupants had left in a hurry.

Had Sheila gotten into Ben's car to go somewhere? Had they gone for help? But if that were the case, wouldn't they have called her back? And why had Sheila disconnected so fast?

Nothing about the situation made sense.

Meredith crept up the stairs, the wood creaking under weight, and peered through the front door. She could now see into the living room, the dining room, and the kitchen. Empty.

It wasn't until she caught sight of the doorframe that she gave pause.

The wood had been splintered and cracked, and it looked like the hinges had been damaged. As if someone — *Ben* — had kicked it in.

Her heart rate increasing, Meredith tried to envision a scenario where breaking down the door would make sense, but came up with nothing. If Ben were inside, he hadn't been invited.

I should call out to Sheila. Let her know that I'm here.

Meredith opened her mouth to speak, but before she could, a bang erupted from upstairs. She jumped back in surprise, raising her hands to defend herself, but there was nothing in front of her.

Get ahold of yourself, Meredith.

The bang came again.

It was coming from one of the rooms upstairs.

She forced herself to move forward. If someone was inside, they might need her help. She walked through the front door and inside, grabbing the rail on the stairs leading to the second floor.

"Sheila? Ben? Everything all right?"

There was no response, but she heard the scurrying sound of footsteps on the floor. Someone was approaching the top landing. Meredith gripped the railing and steeled herself to fight or to talk; whichever the situation called for.

Her hands shook; her fingers were clammy on the rail.

All at once, the footsteps stopped and a head poked around the wall.

Meredith let out a muffled shriek.

It was Sheila.

The old woman lifted her hand to her lips, signaling for Meredith to be quiet, and then waved her up the stairs. Meredith let out a silent sigh of relief, her body still trembling, and then climbed up to meet her.

Thank God she's OK.

When Meredith reached the landing, Sheila clutched her arm with a rigid hand. Although the old woman looked frightened, she looked uninjured: she had sustained no injuries that Meredith could see, and her clothing was intact. In her hands was a rifle.

The old woman pointed to a closed door at the end of the hall.

Meredith nodded and listened. Despite straining her ears, she heard no movement or sound from within. It was almost as if the occupant was listening, too. After a minute of silence, she whispered to the woman next to her.

"Who's in there? Is it Ben?"

The old woman nodded, her lips pursed.

"He's sick," she said simply.

Meredith could make out a light scratch on the other side of the door now, almost as if Ben had heard them. She crept forward a step, then paused.

"Ben? You in there?" she called.

The hallway fell silent. She took another step forward, glancing at the woman next to her. Sheila shook her head, her eyes wide, imploring Meredith to stay put.

"Ben?" she called again. No answer.

Meredith felt her chest tighten, the breakfast she'd eaten that morning starting to travel up her windpipe. She swallowed, forcing it down, and kept her eyes glued to the door.

"Call the police, Sheila," she said.

The old woman handed Meredith the rifle, then padded away, heading down the staircase. Meredith clenched the gun with shaky hands.

If Ben was really inside, she couldn't shoot him, could she? If he was sick, she owed it to him to help.

No sooner had the woman left than the banging erupted again.

Thud-thud-thud.

Meredith watched as the door buckled against its hinges. She stepped back, tripping over a piece of loose carpet, and groped for the wall.

She was still fighting for balance when the door swung open. The wood crashed against the wall, cracking the plaster, and she screamed.

Standing in front of her, eyes blazing, was Ben Sanders.

4

T HINGS WERE EVEN WORSE THAN Dan remembered. As they drove back into St. Matthews — the town that had once been their home — he found that it was barely recognizable. Several days prior, it'd been bad, but nothing like what he saw before him now.

Every window was shattered, every door cracked, and the streets were littered with abandoned vehicles. It was almost as if the town had been hit by a bomb, one that detonated daily and built on the destruction of the day before it. Everywhere Dan looked was a body; everywhere he turned was an obstacle.

He'd given up on asking Quinn to look away. Each time he'd given the warning, her head would swivel as if she had radar, taking in the exact sight he didn't want her to see. It was human nature to be curious, sure, but he couldn't help but think of the mental damage it might be causing her.

No eleven-year-old should have to deal with this.

As he passed through the center of town, he was hit by a wave of memories.

He recognized the turn he'd taken when fleeing the Agents just days earlier. A sandwich shop he'd frequented. The pizza place he took Julie to on their nights out.

He bit his lip.

Although the scenery was worse than before, he was grateful of the knowledge they'd gained since last traveling it. They now knew the root cause of the infection, the perpetrators, and the ways to avoid it.

They'd learned that the virus was ingested, and that it could be avoided by eating the food they'd taken from the agents.

They had a trunk full of safe food, and a destination in mind.

Dan just had to figure a way to get them there.

Without the assistance of GPS or a phone, he'd have to rely on memory alone to take them to Settler's Creek.

As he approached the center of town, the rubble and wreckage began to overtake the road; a few minutes later, he was forced to stop the vehicle. In front of them were two sideways cars, a television set, and a downed street sign.

They were at an impasse.

Dan put the car in reverse, looking for another way around. But when he backed up, he saw that the roads on either side were equally blocked; in some cases, worse than the one he was on.

"Dammit," he said.

Quinn looked over at him.

"Sorry, honey. We'll figure out a way around."

He braced his hands on the wheel and surveyed

the damaged street in front of him. Any time the car wasn't moving, they were in danger of being swarmed by the things.

He'd learned that from experience.

At the same time, there were only a few ways out of town, and if he wanted to get to Oklahoma — and to Meredith's — he'd need to clear the road.

Quinn eyed him nervously from the passenger's seat.

"I don't want you to go out there, Daddy."

"I'm sorry, honey, but I don't have a choice. The street is blocked and I need to clear it."

"Can't we take another road?"

"I don't see any other way around. Don't worry. I'll be quick." He pointed ahead of them to the television and the sign. "If I can move those few things, we can squeeze by on the sidewalk."

Quinn nodded.

"Same drill as before. Keep the windows and doors locked. And take this."

He retrieved the pistol from his holster and placed it on her lap. She held it in her hands nervously. The sight of her holding the loaded weapon still didn't sit well with him, but the prospect of her being defenseless was even worse.

"What about you, Daddy?"

"I'll grab another gun from back," he said. He noticed her face was still filled with doubt. "Don't worry, I'll be careful."

"You promise?"

"I promise."

He managed a smile, hoping to assure her. But the truth was, he was worried. The streets were quiet. Too quiet. He left the keys in the ignition and exited the vehicle, then made his way around to the trunk.

He lifted the hatch, perused the station wagon's contents, and selected a pistol, a Glock 9mm.

After he'd retrieved it, he shut the trunk and signaled for Quinn to lock the doors. The ensuing *click* gave him goose bumps.

If he needed to get back inside, it would take a precious second for his daughter to unlock the doors, and that second could mean the difference between life and death.

He just hoped he didn't have to test the scenario.

Dan tucked the pistol into his holster and walked to the front of the car. The flat-screen television was easy enough to remove. He wrapped his hands around the base, hefted it upwards and out of the vehicle's path, and set it down on the sidewalk.

The sign proved more difficult. The metal was rusted and worn, the pole long and unwieldy. After picking it up, Dan fought for balance; several times he almost dropped it.

He finally managed to carry it onto the sidewalk. He set it on the ground and stepped back to the station wagon.

Before he could get inside, a voice pierced the air.

"Help!"

Dan instinctively reached for his pistol and swiveled to find the source. Was someone still alive out here?

He'd been expecting to encounter one of the creatures while out in the open, maybe even one of the agents. The last thing he'd expected was a survivor.

The cry came again. It sounded like a young female.

It took him a few seconds to pinpoint the person's location. The call of distress was coming from a rooftop across the street. A girl with blonde hair was leaning over the edge, waving both arms in tandem. Her face was fraught with fear, and when she caught Dan's attention, she burst into tears.

"Please don't leave!"

"I won't!" he called up to her.

He found himself slipping into police mode; in seconds, he was running surveillance on the surrounding area, determining the path of least resistance to get to her. There were a few obstacles in his way, but there was no barricade to get to the building she was in; at least none that he could see.

At the same time, there was a good chance that something might be waiting inside.

His eyes darted back to the interior of the station wagon, where Quinn was waiting. She'd spotted the girl, too, and she waved her father onward.

The prospect of leaving his daughter alone made Dan sick to his stomach. At the same time, he knew he couldn't abandon the other survivor. To do that would be to abandon his own humanity, and he wasn't ready to do that.

Not yet.

"Don't move an inch, Quinn! Keep the doors locked!"

She nodded that she understood. Dan drew a breath and then headed across the street to the building.

The building had once been a bank. The exterior was made of brown brick and cement; the roof was square and flat. A covered entrance led to a single door in front. To his surprise, the windows remained intact and the door was shut. It appeared the blonde girl had made the right move in coming inside.

At the same time, he had no idea what might be lurking within.

He made his way across the street, gun drawn, ready to fire at the slightest hint of trouble. The neighboring buildings—a funeral home and a sandwich shop—were dark and demolished, harboring a wealth of shadows. He peered through the broken windows, but could only make out the front half of their interiors.

Where had everyone gone?

Dan found it odd that in just one week, the town could transform from a place of life and color to a place of isolation and emptiness. It was as if the townsfolk had picked up and migrated, tearing the city down behind them.

But somewhere, they had to be here. Even if they'd all been infected, the people of St. Matthews couldn't have just disappeared.

As he approached the door of the bank, he envisioned the things watching his every move, waiting for the chance to pounce. Since leaving the car, he'd felt like there was an invisible spotlight on him, and the feeling gave him chills.

When he reached the bank's entrance, he gave one final glance at the street behind him, then lowered his gun and yanked the handle. The door swung open soundlessly.

He stepped inside.

The world immediately grew a shade darker, and he raised his arms in front of him, training his pistol on the interior.

As he'd expected, the place was in shambles. The countertops were strewn with paperwork, pens, and cups; the office doors left hanging on the hinges. Several bodies were strewn across the floor and countertops.

The smell of death clung to the air, and Dan covered his mouth to repel it.

He stepped through the wreckage, scanning the room for a door that might lead to the roof. Behind the main counter was the vault. Surprisingly, the steel gate was still intact, preventing entry, though it looked like several attempts had been made to open it. He grimaced at a body on the floor next to it. The person's hands were still clinging to the bars, even though their lower half was missing.

To Dan's left was long hallway, which contained a row of glass offices on the left, a set of doors on the right. He crossed the room, heading toward the doors.

Through the glass offices he could see the windows that led to the street. He glanced through them, verifying that his daughter was still safe and sound in the vehicle. When he reached the first door, he tried the handle. The door opened without effort, revealing a host of cleaning supplies: mops, brooms, and buckets. He clicked it closed and tried the other.

The second door contained a flight of stairs, presumably leading to the roof.

He crossed the doorway and started up them.

His footsteps echoed on the stairwell, and he did his best to dampen them, taking one stair at a time. Although the room was dim, he could make out his surroundings from a small window about halfway up the wall.

All clear so far.

At the top was a lone door. He reached for the handle, listening for noise on the other side. If it was indeed the roof, which he assumed it was, then the girl should be waiting for him.

The door wouldn't budge. It was jammed from the other side.

He raised his knuckles and gave it a rap. He heard a feeble voice from the other side, then the sound of objects being moved. The girl must have barricaded herself on the roof. How long had she been up there?

The door handle turned, and he stepped back a few feet.

A face poked through the crack. The girl was pale, fair-skinned, about sixteen years old. Her lips quivered when she took sight of Dan. It looked like she was in a state of shock.

"I thought you were going to leave," she whispered.

The girl kept the door closed to a crack, as if opening it would let in the creatures she'd been trying so hard to keep out. Dan put his hand on the edge of the door.

"Everything's going to be all right," he said. "But we need to get out of here as soon as possible."

She released the door and he parted it the rest of the way, allowing daylight to creep into the stairwell. The girl remained in place. He saw that she was wearing a gray tank top and a pair of tattered white shorts.

"What's your name?"

"Sandy."

He extended his hand.

"I'm Dan Lowery. Listen, Sandy, I know this is difficult, but we really need to get out of here before those things come back."

She glared at his gun, perhaps noticing his stance on the stairwell.

"Are you a police officer?" she asked.

"I was." Dan paused. "But not anymore."

"Who's in the car?"

"My daughter Quinn. You're going to be all right, Sandy. We're going to get you out of here."

No sooner had he spoken the words than she leapt into his arms and started to sob. He embraced her with his free hand, holding her close. He felt awful for the girl. It was as if her entire ordeal had culminated in this moment, and the prospect of escape made it even more real.

He let her cry for a minute, then led her down the stairs one step at a time. He could feel her shaking, and he did his best to console her, keep her quiet.

They were halfway down the stairs when he heard a clatter from somewhere at the bottom. The girl jumped.

"What was that?" she asked.

"I'm not sure."

The two of them halted mid-step. He strained to see the bottom of the stairwell, but the door above them had already shut, pitching them into semi-darkness.

The noise below them continued. It sounded

like it was coming from the main floor of the bank. Dan glanced back at the door to the roof.

"Get ready to run, Sandy."

She clung tighter.

"I'm not going back up there," she whispered.

"Hopefully it won't come to that."

The clatter had increased in volume. It sounded like it was getting closer. Dan's eyes had once again adjusted to the dark; he could now make out the outline of the door below them.

Without warning, it moved, and a hand shimmied through the crack.

Sandy screamed.

Dan cupped his hand over her mouth, but he was too late. The hand retracted and a head came into view, snapping and snarling.

"Back to the roof!" he shouted.

He heard the clap of Sandy's footsteps as she retreated, and then the thud of the door being cast aside. A flood of light penetrated the stairwell, and Dan saw that the creature had wormed its way inside.

He raised his pistol and squeezed off a shot, knocking it backward, but there were already others behind it. Dan tried to determine the exact number, but there were too many to count. The creatures were already climbing the stairs, and with only a limited amount of ammunition, he had no option but to retreat.

He bounded up the stairs and crashed onto the roof, the creatures right on his tail. Sandy was waiting for him. When she saw what was behind him, she clapped her hands against her face.

To his left were a stack of chairs, a couch, and a shelf.

"Quick! Barricade the door!" he yelled.

He slammed it shut behind him, pressing his full weight against it. The door bucked against his shoulder, and he gritted his teeth, doing his best to hold it. Sandy grabbed the couch and began sliding it in place.

But she was too late. The door was already about to give way.

Dan jumped back as a flood of creatures poured from the entrance. He raised his pistol and fired several rounds into the mass, but the numbers were too strong. Before he knew it he was fleeing to the edge of the roof, Sandy behind him.

He peered over the edge, reeling at the sight of the thirty-foot drop and the station wagon below. By his count there were six bullets left in the chamber of his gun—not nearly enough to ward off the horde of creatures in front of them.

"Are there any other weapons up here?" he shouted.

"No!"

The girl behind him was frantic, and she dug her nails into the back of his shirt, as if Dan were the last anchor to her sanity.

He scoured the roof, looking for an escape route. Jumping was out of the question; that was for sure. Other than that, the only other way out that he could see was back through the door they'd come in.

"Dammit!" he yelled.

The creatures were almost upon them, ten feet and closing, and he fired off two shots, felling the two closest to them. No sooner had they fallen than two more emerged to take their place, biting and clawing the air in front of them.

He fixed his eyes on one in particular, which appeared to have been a woman with long dark hair and blue eyes. The creature's face held the same shape and curves as Julie's, and before he knew it, he'd replaced the image with that of his dead wife's.

His heart swelled with despair.

Would he be joining her soon?

Get ahold of yourself, Dan.

The sound of a car door slamming jolted him back to reality.

He looked back over the roof's edge, just in time to see his daughter racing from the station wagon and into the bank.

"Quinn! No!" he shouted.

But he was too late.

His daughter had already entered the building.

5

EREDITH FALTERED BACK DOWN THE hallway, unable to believe what she was seeing. The man coming toward her was pale and disheveled, his eyes rabid and roving. He looked nothing like Ben. His hands raked the air, fingers bloody, and he emitted a low hiss through clenched teeth.

If he recognized Meredith, he showed no outward signs of it. This was not the neighbor she'd known for five years.

This was a different person entirely.

Even still, could she shoot him?

She aimed the rifle at his mid-section, her hands shaking, and wondered if she'd have the courage to pull the trigger.

To be fair, Meredith had known about the infection. She'd seen the details on the news, and she'd even seen footage of the infected. Knowing that things could escalate, that her town could be next, she'd done her best to prepare for the worst. But as she quickly realized, seeing something on the television and seeing it right in front of you were two different things.

There was no way to prepare for something like this.

Ben — or whatever Ben had become — advanced toward her without hesitation, paying little mind to the gun she was carrying, and she backed up several steps until she was next to the stairwell. Her foot slid from the landing onto the first step.

Ben's eyes had stopped roaming, and his gaze locked on her face.

"Ben!" she screamed. "It's me, Meredith!"

But her words were useless. She may as well have been speaking in a foreign language.

She heard a bang from downstairs, and her heart leapt in her chest.

"Sheila? Where are you?" she screamed. But there was no answer from the old woman.

Ben took a swing at her, and she moved to the side, narrowly avoiding him. She moved down another stair and clenched the trigger of the rifle. If she were to run, the man would be upon her in no time; given his size, he'd overtake her in seconds.

Meredith raised her gun; swallowed the lump in her throat.

I'm sorry, Ben.

She squeezed the trigger. The resultant blast knocked her back a step, and she watched as the man stumbled back into the hallway. He hunched over, head tilted to the side, but he did not retreat.

She'd struck him in the arm, and the wound gushed a red spray: a mixture of blood and something else she couldn't identify. Despite the injury, he made no sound, no outward indication that he felt any pain. Instead, he took another plodding step toward her.

Meredith ran.

She took the steps two at a time, her feet sliding across the carpet, and she heard Ben chasing after her. She heard a crash, as if he'd hit the wall, then a series of thuds as his feet hit the stairs.

When she reached the ground floor, she veered right into the kitchen. There was no sign of Sheila, but the phone was lying on the floor. Next to it was a puddle of blood.

"Oh God," Meredith whispered.

Despite her concern, Meredith had no time for hesitation. She heard another enormous crash behind her — probably Ben hitting the first floor landing — and darted through the kitchen and out the open back door.

At the rear of the property was an enormous field. At one time it had been used for growing crops, but with Sheila's husband deceased, it had succumbed to overgrowth. To Meredith's right, fifty feet away, was a barn.

She darted forth without hesitation, her feet pummeling the earth. Although she didn't dare turn around, she could sense Ben's presence behind her. The hissing had increased in volume, and his footfalls thudded against the grass.

The sun blazed overhead, illuminating the field in a golden film. Meredith squinted from the glare. There was still no sign of Sheila. Her hope was that the woman had made it to the barn, that she was waiting for her.

When she was twenty feet from the barn doors, she noticed that they were hanging open. Had Sheila left them ajar? Was the woman in there, bleeding and injured?

Her mind scrambled for answers while her feet traipsed the ground.

She'd almost reached the entrance when she felt something brush the back of her neck. Startled, she tried to pick up speed, but she was too late.

Ben had caught up, and he grabbed ahold of her shirt and flung her to the ground. Meredith pitched forward and onto the dirt, landing on the rifle. The blow knocked the wind out of her, and she struggled to roll over.

Ben was latching on to her legs. She kicked behind her, striking Ben in the face. His grasp relented, and she grabbed hold of the rifle underneath her.

This time she was able to turn around.

She rolled onto her back, propped the gun in front of her, and took sight of her attacker. Ben was still advancing, even though it looked like she'd broken his nose. The same substance that had bled from his arm now erupted from his face, and his eyes were an inky black.

Despite his injuries, he showed no signs of slowing down. He wasn't going to stop until she was dead.

Meredith pulled the trigger, watching the top of his head explode.

His eyes rolled backward, his body crumpled, and Ben fell onto his face.

She stared at him for another minute — this man that had once been her neighbor and friend — and felt a sob rise up in her throat.

How would she explain this to the man's wife? How would she go on living after what she'd done?

Tears sprung to her eyes, and she dropped the rifle in the grass. She'd just killed her neighbor. She was a murderer.

But he wasn't Ben anymore.

Meredith stared at the top of his head, at his pallid, gray arms, and tried to convince herself that she'd done the right thing. Before she could come to any resolution, she heard a commotion coming from the barn.

Sheila.

It wasn't over yet. The woman needed her help. She forced herself to her feet.

Muffled cries wafted from the barn, and she heard a series of scuffs and bangs. From the sounds of it Sheila was in trouble. Meredith retrieved the rifle and dashed the ten feet to the doors, then kicked them open with her foot.

Her stomach instantly dropped.

Lying on her back, stomach torn open, was Sheila Guthright. Sitting on top of her was Ben's wife, Marcy.

6

"MARCY! GET THE HELL OFF of her!" Meredith shouted.

The woman that had once been Marcy snarled, her hands wrapped around the old woman's intestines.

"Now!"

Meredith aimed the gun, her finger on the trigger. Her face was wet with tears, and she fought to control her emotions. In just a few minutes, she'd been forced to kill one of her closest neighbors.

And now she was poised to kill another.

Marcy hissed at her, holding up her blood-laced fingers as if to taunt Meredith. She lowered her hands back to Sheila's stomach, ready to continue her parade of gore, but before she could, Meredith fired.

The gunshot echoed through the barn.

Marcy fell sideways, collapsing like a stone.

Meredith dropped the rifle to the dirt and rushed to the old woman's aid. Sheila opened her mouth, emitting a trickle of blood. Her stomach had been torn open, her insides torn and upended.

"Stay still," Meredith instructed.

Tears streamed down her face. Without being

a doctor, she knew that the woman was mortally wounded. The nearest hospital was about fifty miles away. Even if they could make it, she doubted the woman would survive.

But she'd try to nonetheless.

"I'll be right back, Sheila. I promise."

Meredith raced out of the barn, past the bodies of Marcy and Ben, and across the field. Her throat was tight and constricted, and her pulse still raced, but this time for a different reason.

Two of her neighbors were dead, and another was dying.

The kitchen was even worse than she had left it. The chairs had been knocked over, the door hung off its hinges. Ben had torn through it like a whirlwind, destroying everything in his path to get to her.

She'd been extremely lucky.

She just wished she'd reached Sheila earlier, before Marcy had —

Meredith pushed the thought from her mind and picked up the phone. She clicked the button off, then on again. The receiver spit a dial tone. She tapped the numbers 9-1-1 and waited for the phone to connect.

But it didn't.

It rang and rang.

That's impossible, she thought. *How could nobody be there?*

But she knew the reason, and try as she might, she was unable to ignore it. She hung up and dialed again, same result. Frantic now, she tried the phone numbers of her closest neighbors. No matter whom she called, she was unable to get a response.

The fear inside her grew.

How could things have happened so fast?

She looked at her hands as if expecting herself to suddenly transform, but her fingers remained fleshy and white. She'd been careful not to consume anything other than what was on her farm. Had Ben and Marcy done the same? She thought they had, but she couldn't be sure.

Meredith left the phone behind and raced back out the kitchen door. Once outside, she glanced at the driveway. Her car was still adjacent to the house, a hundred feet away.

She changed course from the barn to her car. She could still make out the body of Ben Parsons on the ground, and as she ran, she had the sudden premonition that the man would sit up and chase her. But he remained still.

When she reached her truck, she jumped in, started the engine, and drove up to the barn's entrance. If Meredith couldn't get ahold of an ambulance, she'd drive Sheila to the hospital herself.

She darted back into the barn.

Sheila's eyes were half-closed and her breathing was shallow.

"Stay with me, Sheila!" she shouted.

She glanced at the woman's stomach, where

blood was still spilling from inside, creating a puddle on the dirt beside her. Meredith had never seen so much blood in her life. She gritted her teeth and looked for a towel.

I need to stop the bleeding. Put pressure on it. Then I can move her.

The rational part of her mind told her that her efforts would be useless, that no matter what she did, the woman was already on a one-way trip to death's door. But Meredith ignored the thoughts and continued, refusing to give up.

Finding nothing in the barn, she raced back for the house, intent on retrieving a clean towel to apply to the wound. She crashed through the kitchen and into the bathroom, and whipped open the closet. Inside were several clean towels. She tucked them under her armpit and darted back for the barn.

When she got to Sheila's side, her heart dropped even further. The old woman's eyes were rolled back in her head, and she'd stopped breathing.

Meredith placed her fingers on the woman's neck, but there was no sign of life, no pulse. She placed her hands on the woman's chest, right above the gaping wound, and started chest compressions. Every few seconds she held her ear to the woman's mouth, hoping to resuscitate her.

Blood soaked her hands, and the woman's frail body seemed to cave underneath her touch. After a few seconds she stopped.

There was no use. Try as she might, there was nothing she could do. Sheila Guthright was dead.

Meredith covered her face with her hands and sobbed into the empty barn.

7

DAN RAISED HIS PISTOL AT the creatures on the roof, ready to expend his last few rounds of ammunition. Sandy crouched behind him. If he had to guess, there were about ten of the things in front of him: no matter how good his aim was, he wouldn't be able to hit them all. His only option was to incapacitate as many as he could and try to create an opening.

He trained his gun on the closest creature—a man with an unkempt bloodied beard and flannel shirt—and squeezed off a round into its head. The thing staggered back, bumping into two others behind it and collapsing to the pavement. Dan swiveled to his left, shooting a woman-creature with long dark hair, and then fired two more rounds into two things behind it.

He continued to fire until his gun clicked empty and he was out of ammunition. He'd managed to fell about six of the creatures. There were still four remaining, and they charged at him with mouths agape.

Among them were two males and two females; all were equidistant from where he stood.

He lashed out with his foot, catching one of the males in the ankle, sending it toppling downward, then struck another male in the face with his fist. The creature's cheek was cold and hard, and the impact jarred his knuckles.

In spite of the pain, he kept on. The things had pressed Sandy and him backward so they were only a few feet from the edge of the roof: if they weren't mauled first, they were destined to fall.

He needed to create a diversion, an opening.

"Get ready to run!" he shouted to Sandy.

One of the creatures lunged at Dan — a woman in a floral-print dress — and he grabbed it by the fabric and flung it from the roof. Of the three creatures remaining, only one was on its feet.

"Go!" he yelled to Sandy.

The girl darted from behind him, making a beeline for the entrance.

The last female latched onto his arm.

Dan wrenched himself away and took a step closer to the edge of the roof. Out of the corner of his eye, he could see the pavement looming thirty feet below. He attempted to sidestep, but the two things on the ground had recovered, and the three creatures had walled him in.

There was nowhere to go.

He covered his head with his hands, trying to push his way between them, but none budged. Hot breath filled the air above, drawing closer, and he thrashed his arms to no avail.

Was this the end? After all they'd been through, would this be his demise?

He'd almost given up when a familiar voice rang out across the rooftop.

"Dad! Duck!"

Dan dropped to the ground. Gunshots rocked the air above him, and he pressed himself against the asphalt. One by one the creatures collapsed on top of him, crushing him in a tangle of limbs. He wrenched his body from side to side, doing his best to free himself.

This time he was able to fling them off.

He emerged from the heap and stared at his daughter's frail form across the rooftop.

In her hands was the pistol he'd given her.

"Quinn!"

She lowered the gun. Sandy was standing behind her. Both of them appeared unharmed.

He sprang across the rooftop, covering the gap between them, and held his daughter close. She handed him the weapon.

"Are you mad at me?" she asked.

"For what?"

"Leaving the car."

"Not at all. Thank God you did," he said. "I'm not sure what I would've done otherwise."

He glanced over at Sandy, who was still shaking. He opened his arms and embraced her as well.

"Now let's all get the hell out of here."

Three pairs of footsteps clapped the stairwell as the survivors made their way down it, hands linked in a human chain. The bank had returned to silence.

When they reached the bottom of the stairwell, Dan paused, halting them with an upturned hand. Beneath them were the bodies of the creatures he'd shot earlier. He scanned the lifeless limbs, certain that one would spring to life, but all remained still.

He cracked the door.

The main floor of the bank was dark and dismal, empty, but he knew it wouldn't stay that way for long. Chances were that the commotion had roused other things in the area and they'd be coming soon.

"Come on," he hissed.

He led the pair through the bank, stepping over the paperwork and debris he'd traversed just minutes earlier. To his right were the glass offices and windows. He kept one eye trained on the outside.

When they were halfway across the bank, he saw movement outside.

Dan paused mid-step.

"What is it?" Quinn whispered.

He put his finger to his lips, waited. The movement was coming from a bakery across the street. Inside the building, he could see several smashed coolers, a table and chairs, and a counter. Everything beyond that was black. He strained his eyes, but none of the shadows changed shape and nothing moved.

"I'm not sure. Let's go. Carefully."

He pulled them onward. When they reached the front door, he inched it open with his forearm. The road in front of them was deserted. The station wagon was parked just as he'd left it, a blue beacon in an otherwise demolished landscape.

Dan pushed the door open the remainder of the way. The hinges squeaked, echoing into the street and the surrounding buildings. Without the hum of electricity or the din of traffic, the entire city had become a conduit for sound, and he shuddered at the disturbance.

Before they could proceed, footsteps sounded, and he pushed the girls back inside.

He pressed his back against the open door. The beat grew louder. Clutching the pistol between his palms, he snuck a glance into the street.

To his surprise, the source was immediately apparent. Rather than one of the creatures, the footsteps belonged to a man.

The man was running in a full sprint down the middle of the street. He was wearing a black jean jacket and dark jeans, sporting a thick shock of black hair and several days worth of scruff. Dan knew the man from town—he'd been arrested multiple times for theft. The man's name was Reginald Morris. By the looks of it, the man had somehow survived the infection.

But what was he doing out in the open, and why was he running?

And more importantly, what was he running *from*?

Dan stuck his head back out in the open, but saw nothing in pursuit of the man. Reginald had quickly closed the gap between the bakery and the front of the bank. His feet pounded the pavement, and his breathing was loud and uneven.

The man threw a glance over his shoulder, then at the bank, locking eyes with Dan.

"Reginald!"

Dan stepped out into the open and waved his hands, but the man continued, ignoring his cry. Reginald tore up alongside the station wagon, tried the handle, and flung open the door. Then he jumped inside.

"What're you doing?" Dan shouted.

Dan dashed into the street, frantically trying to stop the man, but it was too late. The door locks had already clicked shut and Reginald had started the engine.

Before Dan could react, the man peeled off down the street, leaving a plume of exhaust in his wake.

Quinn and Sandy ran up behind him, both of them yelling as well.

Dan wiped his hands across his face, resisting the urge to scream out in frustration. Even if he did, there'd be no one to blame but himself.

He'd left the keys in the car on purpose, to

allow his daughter a means of escape should something happen to him. He'd had no idea that she would end up leaving the car, no idea that she wouldn't think to take the keys.

More importantly, he couldn't have predicted that another survivor would stumble across them, using the opportunity to rob them of the only thing in the world they had left.

It was a chain of events that, in retrospect, could only be credited to bad luck.

Dammit.

"What are we going to do?" Quinn whispered.

He hesitated.

"We need something else to drive."

The task would be a lot more difficult than it sounded. By the looks of it, many of the vehicles had been damaged or crashed. Of those that were untouched, not all of them had keys. Even if they were to procure another vehicle, they'd lost their entire stock of uncontaminated food and drink.

Dan struggled to keep his composure.

"We'd better get moving," he said.

Before he could take a step, Sandy stopped him.

"I know where he's going."

"Who?"

"Reginald. The man who stole your car."

"You know him?"

"Yes. He's one of the survivors I've been staying with."

Dan eyed her with suspicion. "Why didn't you

say something earlier? Why didn't you yell out to him?"

"I tried, but it all happened so fast. If he'd seen me, I'm sure he wouldn't have driven off. He probably came looking for me."

"Do you know where he went?"

"Yes. He would've driven back to the lumberyard."

"Is that where you've been staying?"

"Yes."

"How many of you are there?"

"Ten."

Sandy looked at him, her eyes tearing up.

"I had no idea Reginald would do this. We all agreed that if we found more survivors, we'd do our best to help them. I can't believe he stranded us."

Dan sighed. "I'm not surprised. In fact, I know Reginald pretty well myself."

He briefed the two of them on Reginald's background, as well as the man's run-ins with the law.

"I only met him two days ago," Sandy said. "He seemed nice enough. This is my fault. If I hadn't gotten stuck up there—"

"Don't worry about it, Sandy. We'll get the car back. The lumberyard is only a twenty-minute walk from here. We'll just have to be careful."

He glanced down the street, which was still devoid of movement. Even though the area appeared to be clear, he knew it was far from safe.

Given the noise they'd created — both from their encounter with the creatures and their encounter with Reginald — Dan was certain more things would be right around the corner.

As if on cue, a series of crashes erupted from the adjacent block.

He motioned the girls onward.

"Let's go. There's no time to waste."

8

MEREDITH STARED AT THE THREE bodies on the ground in front of her. After Sheila passed, she'd covered them with sheets, placing them next to each other in the barn. It seemed like the decent thing to do.

The last thing she wanted was for the animals to get at them.

In a normal situation—if a situation like this could ever be called normal—she would have left the bodies in place and waited for the police. But the circumstances were far from normal, and her instincts told her help wouldn't be coming soon.

She wasn't sure if it would ever come.

Meredith staggered outside into the field, letting the warm sun glance off her face. For a moment, she convinced herself that all of this was imagined, that she was lying in bed, about to awaken.

But each time she glanced back into the barn, the sheets were still there, and so were the people underneath.

Her closest neighbors—Ben, Marcy, and Sheila—were all dead, and Meredith was alone.

She wandered back into Sheila's house in a daze, her mind still reeling, and stepped through the kitchen and into the living room. On top of an antique-looking table was an equally old-looking television, and she hit the power button and turned it on.

Static.

She hit the channel buttons, flipping from station to station, but came across nothing but black and white fuzz. Gone were the newscasters with their warnings and speculations, gone were the televangelists with their prophecies of doom.

It was as if Meredith was the last person on earth.

She turned off the set and walked back to the phone, once again dialing every number she could think of. The phone rang and rang.

She hung up the receiver, hands trembling. After a few seconds, she wandered over to the window.

Meredith could see the road from here. The asphalt was long, flat, and empty. Not a car going in either direction. If something widespread were happening, wouldn't she see someone trying to escape? Wouldn't someone eventually drive by?

The only thing she could think of was that they were all stuck in a situation like her. Either they were infected, or they were being attacked by someone who was.

The thought made her shudder.

Regardless of where everyone was, there must be police *somewhere*. And even if they were preoccupied, she needed to let them know what had happened.

She glanced over at the front door, which was still hanging open from where Ben had crashed into it. A breeze had begun to blow over the fields, and the door creaked on its broken hinge, swaying back and forth in the gentle air.

She dug out her car key and walked toward it.

The center of town was a few miles away.

Her best option—her only option—was to head to Settler's Creek and look for help. There were bound to be people there. There had to be. She'd find whomever she could, then locate the police and tell them what happened.

She'd made it halfway across the living room when she paused. If she were going into town, she'd need a weapon.

"The rifle," she said aloud.

She doubled back outside and to the barn.

The rifle lay right where she had left it, and she picked it up, carrying it with her. She'd only gotten as far as the door when she thought of something. In the time she'd collected the rifle and headed for the door, a name had crossed her mind.

John Parish.

Of all the phone numbers she'd dialed, his hadn't been among them.

It'd been six months since they had seen each other, and even longer since they'd spoken. Their breakup hadn't exactly been on the best of terms.

Still, regardless of what had transpired between them, shouldn't she at least try to call him?

What if John was there? What if he needed help?

She gripped the rifle in her hands, still wrestling with the idea, and strode toward the pickup. Even under these circumstances, the thought of phoning him had her stomach twisted in knots.

She pictured his chiseled face, his dark hair, the hint of stubble that seemed to be permanently affixed to his cheeks. She'd fallen for him. Hard.

And he'd done nothing but betray her.

She thrust the image of his face from her mind, continuing toward the vehicle. His store was located right on the edge of town, about fifteen minutes away. She'd have to pass by it on the way in. If he were there, she'd stop and make sure he was ok.

But what if he was in trouble now?

Meredith's stopped mid-stride. Before she knew it, she'd detoured past the truck and ran the front door.

She would dial his number once. Make sure he was all right. He probably wouldn't answer anyway. Nobody else had.

She snagged the receiver from the wall and punched the numbers by heart; surprised she still remembered them.

How could I forget?

The phone was silent for a minute as it connected.

The dead air felt like an eternity.

Finally, the other line rang, and she could feel her fingers shaking on the hard plastic, her heart thudding in her chest.

Would it be worse if John answered, or worse if he didn't? What would she say to him?

She pressed the phone to her ear, afraid that she might miss his greeting. The phone rang and rang.

On the sixth ring — just as she was about to hang up — someone answered.

"Hello?"

The voice on the other end was hoarse, barely audible.

"John?"

"Meredith? Is that you?"

His voice wavered as he spoke, and she could hear banging and clattering in the background.

"Are you all right? What's all that noise?"

"I tried calling you..." His voice trailed off.

"I'm not at home. I'm at Sheila Guthright's house. Something happened to her, John. She's been — "

A crash sounded from the other end of the phone, and Meredith jumped in surprise, almost dropping the receiver.

"John, what's going on over there?"

"Meredith...there's something I need to tell you..."

The noise had risen to a crescendo; John's voice was barely audible. Meredith clutched the phone tight, suddenly terrified that she'd lose contact with him.

"John? What is it? Can you hear me? I need you to stay on the phone."

A hiss washed over the other end, drowning out the man's response. Meredith's heart hammered, and she screamed his name into the mouthpiece.

"John! Don't hang up!"

All at once the noise subsided. She strained her ears, waiting for the man to speak again, but all she could hear was the sound of him breathing on the other end. Finally he spoke.

"I've always loved you, Meredith," he said.

There was a gunshot, and then the phone disconnected.

PART TWO

THE NORTH STAR

9

DAN, QUINN, AND SANDY NAVIGATED the streets soundlessly, deadening their footsteps as they walked. The town contained an eerie calm, as if the three of them were on stage, an invisible audience watching from the shadows.

Aside from the pack of creatures they'd seen inside the bank, they'd yet to see any others, and the quietude was making Dan nervous. Every now and again he'd hear a distant crash or a footfall, but each time nothing appeared.

It was as if the creatures were biding their time, waiting for the right moment to strike.

The three of them were currently on Vanderbilt Street, an offshoot of the main road that ran through St. Matthews. All around them were brick commercial buildings and small service shops. Despite his ten years in the community, Dan realized he'd never paid much attention to them. Now it seemed like they were impossible to ignore.

To his right were a vacuum cleaner store, a woodworking company, and a jewelry maker. To his left a salon, an art gallery, and a historical museum.

It was as if these places hadn't even existed

before today, and had sprung to life only to complete the picture of the perfect town.

And St. Matthews *had* been the perfect town. Or pretty damn close to it.

Sure, the town had had its problems. But the good had usually outweighed the bad. Dan had never regretted his decision to move to St. Matthews, and he was sure Julie hadn't, either.

Together they'd built a life here, providing a stable home for Quinn and working in professions that were satisfying and rewarding.

Now, the town was a grim reminder of a life torn apart. Not just for him, but for the several thousand other residents who once lived here.

It was time to get out. There was nothing left for them here.

Dan crept through the broken street, keeping a cautious eye on his surroundings. Each new block presented a host of dark hiding places, and he did his best to scrutinize every one. Behind him, Quinn and Sandy had linked hands, and he could hear their bated breath as they walked the pavement.

Ahead of him were cars spun sideways, signs bent and hanging over, and a slew of paperwork and discarded clothing. There were also bodies — some sitting upright in vehicles, as if they might fire the engines and drive away — others lying in the middle of the street. Unlike a few days prior, the bodies had started to decompose, their limbs picked at by the birds.

So far, the cars they'd seen had been crashed, but Dan kept his eyes peeled for a vehicle they could use. Being on foot made him feel open and exposed, and the feeling was unsettling.

They'd already travelled several blocks from the bank; the lumberyard was a few miles away. If they could reach it without incident, he'd persuade Reginald to return their car, either by conversation or by force.

Whatever it took.

Dan peered into a pickup truck on the side of the road. The windows were smashed and the airbag deflated. By the looks of it, the truck had crashed into an older-model Buick, and the Buick sat empty at the side of the road. Unlike the pickup, the Buick appeared intact, sporting only a dent in the rear bumper.

Dan crept to the driver's side window and peered in. A set of keys dangled from the ignition. The only passenger was a body in the passenger's seat.

The girls had stopped behind him, and they stared, awaiting direction.

He held up his pointer finger.

"Hold on," he mouthed.

The window of the vehicle was rolled up. The driver's door was locked, but he could see an open window on the other side. He made his way over.

Once on the other side, he reached over the sill into the passenger's seat, avoiding the lifeless body that resided there. The corpse was a woman's, and her bloodied, matted hair reminded him of the bristles of a broom. Her face was sunken in and gray, her features obscured by the onset of decay.

Dan hit a button and unlocked the doors.

The *click* made him jump, and he stared over his shoulder at the street, certain he'd have awoken something nearby. The coast was clear.

The girls stood at the trunk of the car, doe-eyed and nervous, and he gave them a nod for reassurance. Then he reached across the lap of the dead woman and turned the key.

The engine rumbled and fired.

"Let's go, girls," he said. "In the backseat."

Given the noise of the vehicle, they had to leave. At the same time, he didn't want to ride with a dead body. He ripped open the passenger's side door and grabbed hold of the dead woman, intending to place her in the street.

To his dismay, the woman's clothing snagged; despite his efforts, he was unable to move her. It took him a minute to realize she had her seatbelt on.

"Jesus Christ," he muttered.

The girls had already scooted into the rear of the vehicle and were watching him, hands clutching the seats. Out of the corner of his eye, he saw Quinn glancing out the back window. He continued to tug at the body.

"Dad!" she yelled suddenly.

His fingers froze on the seatbelt latch, and

he followed her gaze. It didn't take him long to notice what she'd seen.

The street behind them had filled with creatures.

Moans and footfalls filled the air, a cavalcade of the things tumbling forward over cars and debris to get to them. There was no time to delay.

Dan clambered over the woman's body and pulled the door shut behind him. When he reached the driver's seat, he kicked away a pile of papers and trash underfoot and found the gas pedal.

Then he put the vehicle into drive.

The Buick hesitated, and for a split second, Dan feared that it was more damaged than he thought. *Come on, dammit.* He pushed the pedal to the floor. A second later the car lurched forward and out into the road, and he wrenched the steering wheel away from the curb.

In the rearview, he saw that the creatures had gained ground; a few had managed to grip the trunk, their fingernails sliding across the metal. Dan accelerated and swerved around an abandoned vehicle, effectively throwing them off, and proceeded up the road.

The streets had come alive.

Creatures sprang from the windows, emerged through alleyways, and crashed through doors. It was as if the Buick had become a signal, emitting an invisible beacon to the world around it. The clutter on the road thickened, and without warning, Dan's speed fell to a crawl.

The things poured from all sides now, converging on the vehicle. One of them flung itself into the open passenger's side window, dangling halfway over the sill.

Dan hit the automatic window lever, lifting the pane on its midsection. The window gears ground as they strained against the weight of the creature.

"Dad!"

Hands pounded the Buick on all sides, and despite his efforts, Dan struggled to keep his focus on driving. In spite of that, he knew he couldn't give up. The girls in the backseat were depending on him.

The creature in the window snapped its jaws, trying to reach Dan. Raising the window had only trapped it; now it was stuck between the window and the doorframe.

"Is there anything you can use back there to hit it?" he shouted.

The girls dug under the seats behind him. Dan reached for the pistol tucked in his pants, but the creature had begun to swat at him, as if sensing what he had in store.

"I've got something!" Sandy yelled.

Dan's eyes flicked to the rearview; the girl had found a crowbar. He watched as she leaned over the seat and started clubbing the thing. The creature spit and flailed.

"I'm going to roll down the window! When I do, hit it as hard as you can!"

"OK!" the girl cried.

He jabbed the button, lowering the window, and watched as Sandy swung at the thing's skull. The crowbar connected with its forehead, and it fell limp into the passenger's seat, resting on top of the dead woman.

Dan swerved left and then right, shaking it loose, and it toppled backward and fell out into the street. He rolled up the window, just in time to avoid another pair of lunging hands.

The creatures in the street had thickened — there were now several hordes approaching from the front. So far Dan had been able to drive unimpeded, but the road was getting worse. Up ahead, a minivan and a dump truck barred the majority of the street, and the sidewalk wasn't looking much better.

Despite his practiced driving skills, there was only so much Dan could do.

He withdrew the gun Quinn had used and set it on his lap. If he'd counted correctly, there were five bullets left. The rest of their weapons had been stolen with the station wagon.

He glared at the grim path ahead of them, looking for options.

The sidewalk was covered in restaurant furniture, trees, and newspaper boxes. Even if he were to veer onto it, they wouldn't make it more than a few feet. At the same time, the road ahead was completely blocked off.

He had to do something. The creatures had them surrounded.

"Hang on!" he shouted.

Eyeing the two tear-stained faces in the backseat, Dan swerved off the road, heading straight for the nearest building.

MEREDITH BIT BACK THE TEARS. She clenched the phone in her hand, dialing John's number over and over, but it was useless. There was no answer. After the fourth try she let the receiver drop and grabbed her rifle.

She needed to get to him. Fast.

She darted back out the door, feet pounding the grass, and jumped inside her pickup. The engine growled. She revved the gas and spun the tires, doing a U-turn on the field, then roared down the driveway.

When she reached the end, she barreled onto the main road without stopping.

She thought back to what she'd heard. There had been noises; of that she was certain. Someone or some*thing* had been in John's store, or trying to break in. That alone had her panicked. But even more troubling was the single gunshot. That was enough to make her stomach feel queasy, hollow inside.

She just hoped to God he was all right.

In spite of what John had done to her, she couldn't deny what they'd once had. She'd repressed her feelings for months, trying to forget this man, but now that he was in danger her emotions had come back stronger than ever.

Before the phone disconnected, John had said that he loved her. And try as she might, Meredith couldn't deny the fact that she loved him, too.

Meredith had first met John on a trip to town about a year ago.

She'd been driving to the market, intent on getting the week's groceries, when she saw a sign on the side of the road that she'd never seen before.

"Furniture Shop."

The sign was simple and plain, propped against a wooden barrel in the parking lot of a small log-cabin storefront. Formerly the building had been used to house one of the local farmer's vegetables, but it hadn't been occupied in years. For as long as she could remember, it'd been boarded up and closed down.

Driving by that day, she'd been surprised to find the building open, the doors ajar and the lights on inside. A blue pickup had been sitting in the gravel parking lot, a Michigan license plate on the back.

After driving several miles past the store, Meredith's curiosity had gotten the better of her, and she'd driven back and pulled in. Then she'd cut the engine and stepped out into the parking lot.

Aside from her car and the blue pickup, the place had been deserted. She'd walked in with a furrowed brow, unsure of what she'd find inside.

True to the sign out front, the store had been filled with furniture: chairs, tables, dressers, and bureaus. Many were plain wood, unstained, and several were still in progress. It appeared all the furniture had been built by hand.

The shop was comprised of one large room, with several support beams in the center to solidify the structure. There was a door in back, but it was closed, and as far as she knew there were no other buildings behind it.

After perusing the contents of the shop for a few minutes with no sign of the owner, she'd forced a cough, hoping to announce her presence. It was then that she'd heard the noise coming from out back — a slow, rhythmic scraping coming from behind the shop.

Meredith had walked out of the store and made her way around back. The area around the furniture shop was covered in field grass, with no other buildings in sight. If it weren't for the several stores that she knew were about a mile down the road, it would almost feel like the building had been transplanted from somewhere else, thrust into nature without forethought.

When she reached the back of the store, she saw a figure in the distance — a man bent over a piece of wood, his arms moving in a repeated pattern. As she walked closer, she could see that he was using a hand plane.

She was ten feet away before he noticed her. When he did, he jumped.

"Hi," Meredith said sheepishly. "I didn't mean to scare you."

The man set down the plane and smiled.

"That's OK. I needed a break anyway."

He rose to his feet to greet her, dusting his palms on his jeans.

Meredith noticed several things at the same time: he was a lot taller than her, he was in great shape, and he was handsome. Before she knew it she was blushing, and she took a few awkward steps forward to meet his hand.

"I'm Meredith Tilly."

"John Parish," he said.

With the introductions over with, she shoved her hands in her jeans pockets, hoping he wouldn't see her shaking. Normally Meredith was outgoing and relaxed, but something about him had her off her game.

"I love the store. When did you open?"

"Today, actually."

"Really?"

"Yep. You're my first customer." This time it was his turn to blush.

"Hopefully I'll be the first of many."

John smiled.

"Where'd you move from?" she asked, recalling the Michigan license plate.

"Detroit."

"That's a long ways from Settler's Creek, Oklahoma. How'd you end up here?"

John shrugged.

"This place isn't exactly a commercial hotbed," she said.

She immediately clasped her hand over her mouth.

"I'm sorry. That might have come out wrong. I guess I'm just surprised that you'd choose our little town."

John laughed. "I know. I just wanted a change of pace. This is actually a lifelong dream of mine, believe it or not. I've been building kitchens and wall units for years, but I've always wanted to run my own furniture shop. I passed through here on a road trip a while back and I fell in love."

"I'm sure you'll do great here." She smiled.

"Thanks. My plan is to manufacture most of my furniture here and then sell it at local shows and conventions."

"I assume everything here is handmade?" she asked.

"Yep. And if you don't see something here that you'd like, I'd be happy to build it for you."

"I might take you up on that. I'm actually in the market for a new kitchen table and chairs."

Meredith flashed a smile. In truth, she didn't need a kitchen set, because she rarely had visitors.

The furniture she had was in decent enough shape, and besides, she didn't have the extra money to be spending on something like that.

After a few more minutes of small talk, she'd shaken his hand and parted ways with the shop owner.

A week later she'd gone back and placed an order.

Things with John had heated up quickly. Before Meredith knew it, she'd been at his shop almost every day with a new question about her kitchen set. He'd always done his best to answer her, offering suggestions about the wood and the stains, explaining the process as he built it.

After discussing her order, they would go on to talk about a host of other things: news about town, Meredith's farm, or books and movies they'd enjoyed. Like her, John was an avid reader, and they soon discovered that they liked many of the same novels.

John also told her about life in Detroit. He'd said that he'd lived there his whole life, but he'd always hated the city. When he was twenty-two, he'd taken a bicycle across the country by himself, taking in the sights and sounds of all the states he'd never seen. And though he'd appreciated the coasts, he'd always had a soft spot for the Midwest.

Meredith had told him all about her childhood on the farm—how she'd inherited it from her parents when they passed away, how she'd been working there ever since. She'd always wanted to travel, she'd said, but she hadn't had the chance.

"Maybe we could travel together someday," John had said.

The two had laughed at the thought. A few moments later they'd kissed.

They'd been inseparable after that. When she wasn't running the farm, Meredith would visit John at the furniture shop, and when he wasn't building furniture, John was helping Meredith in the fields.

Despite their budding relationship, there'd been no talk of anything further. Each remained in their respective homes, living in tandem, enjoying the time they were spending together.

The people in town had been happy for them. Meredith's friends had only kind words to say about John, and she'd found herself happier than she'd been in a while.

Until six months ago when everything changed.

Meredith had been visiting John at the furniture shop when it happened. Per her usual routine, she'd brought him a late breakfast of fresh-cooked eggs and toast. She'd always enjoyed seeing him in the late morning—Meredith was an early riser. After taking care of her harvesting before sunrise, by eleven o'clock she was ready for a break. And though the meals she brought John were often cold, he'd never complained.

On that day, John had been working on a custom rocking chair for Mrs. Ashby, one of the elder residents of the town. Upon seeing Meredith, he'd stopped what he was doing and joined her in the shop, happily devouring his breakfast.

They'd been talking about a movie when someone walked in behind them. Meredith had been facing the back wall; John had been facing the entrance. Although Meredith hadn't seen the woman at first, she'd seen the expression change on John's face.

His mouth had hung open, and he'd dropped his plate on the floor.

"Hello, Eve," he'd said.

Meredith had swiveled in her chair, suddenly facing a woman with straight, dark hair and pursed lips. The woman was wearing a stylish black blouse, a gray skirt, and carried a designer purse. She didn't look like anyone Meredith recognized.

"Who's this?" Meredith had asked.

Both John and the woman had stared at her. After a few seconds, John had answered, his face beet red.

"This is my wife."

11

FTER STORMING OUT OF THE furniture shop, Meredith had jumped into her pickup and peeled out of the parking lot. Tears had been streaming down her face; a pit had taken root in her stomach.

John had lied to her. In the months she'd known him, he'd never mentioned having a wife. Even when he talked about Detroit, he'd never alluded to the fact that he was married, or even that he'd been dating.

It was as if he'd carefully omitted that detail, hoping that Meredith would never find out. The thought had made her sick. What else had he lied about? Was John even his real name?

Regardless of who John was or what else he'd lied about, Meredith had vowed one thing: she'd never talk to John Parish again.

Over the next few weeks John had called her repeatedly, even stopping by her house several times. Each time she'd refused to speak with him.

Eventually he'd left a letter in the mailbox.

According to the letter, John had been separated from his wife for over a year, and until recently, he'd had no idea where she was or what she was doing. He said he'd wanted to tell Meredith, but was afraid of how she'd react.

Meredith didn't know what to believe. Even if the letter was true, John had destroyed her trust, and to her, trust was everything. He should've told her the truth from the beginning. He shouldn't have lied.

Weeks passed, and after a while, John stopped trying to contact her. Even still, Meredith had gone out of her way to avoid the furniture shop, taking a detour of several miles so as not to see him when she went into town.

Despite her anger, she'd never mentioned anything to her friends or neighbors. She'd always believed in privacy, and her love life was her business. Besides, Meredith was ashamed. She'd been lied to and deceived, and she was deeply hurt and embarrassed.

As the months wore on, Meredith began to move forward. She resumed her normal route to town, and though she tried not to look over, she still saw John's blue truck in the gravel lot. Occasionally she'd even catch a glimpse of him through the open front doors, arranging his wares or working on his latest piece of furniture.

But she'd never stopped. Not even once.

Now, as she drove down the rural road, she realized all that was about to change. The world was a different place, and John was in trouble.

No matter what he had done to her, he needed

help. And that took precedence over anything that might've happened between them.

Meredith sank the gas pedal to the floor, propelling her pickup faster than she'd driven in years. Fields whipped past her, and the road hummed beneath her tires. If she didn't reach John soon, she might not make it in time to help him.

She might be too late already.

Back at Sheila's house, she'd gotten a taste of what she was up against, but that was nothing compared to what she assumed was out there. It'd been difficult enough fighting for her life against Ben and Marcy; she couldn't imagine it getting any worse.

The furniture shop was only a few miles away. Before she knew it, she'd rounded the last curve that stood between her and the building. She could see the building on the horizon now — a square, wooden structure that dotted the landscape. From here, everything looked just as she remembered it. She could even decipher the outline of John's blue pickup in front of the store.

Please God let him be all right.

She repeated the words in her head, her stomach turned upside down with nerves.

When she got closer, her heart began to hammer. There was movement outside the building. Too much movement. She squinted her eyes and lowered the visor, hoping what she was seeing wasn't real. At the same time, she knew that it was.

The furniture shop was surrounded by a mob of people.

About thirty people — *infected* people — crowded the walls, banging and kicking to get inside. Hands and limbs flailed, and bodies toppled over one another. Above it all, a chorus of moans and hisses wafted into the air, sending needles of fear through Meredith's body.

She weaved to a stop in front of the building, leaving a thirty-foot buffer zone between the vehicle and the horde, and fumbled for the rifle. When she had it in her hands, she reached for the door handle. Then she stopped short.

What was she planning to do? With that many of the infected, her weapon was as good as useless. She only had a few rounds left, at best — certainly not enough to combat all of them.

She leaned her head out the window and screamed.

"John! Are you in there? Yell back so I can hear you!"

She paused, giving him a chance to respond. The noise from the infected increased in volume, and several of them turned to face her. She saw several feet starting to trudge toward her, and she transitioned her foot from the brake to the gas.

"John!"

There was still no sign of the man, and no response.

A handful of the creatures were running in her direction now, and she stomped the gas, kicking up gravel behind her. The truck rolled across the loose stone; the infected grew closer.

Maybe if I can lure them away...

She flung the rifle on the seat and hit her horn. Once. Twice. Three times.

More of the infected peeled themselves from the walls of the furniture shop, joining the others in pursuit of the pickup. She hit the horn again, but this time she held it down, the tone blaring into the air and drowning out the sounds of the creatures.

The forerunners of the group were within feet of the vehicle, and she hit the gas and sped back toward the road, keeping one step ahead of them. The things faltered and fell as they lunged for the bed of the vehicle.

"Come on!" she screamed as she diverted them from the building.

She stared in the rearview at the furniture shop, but there was still no indication that John had heard her, or even that he was alive. Almost all of the creatures had fled the structure.

Having successfully gained their attention, she toggled the gas and brake, leading them step-by-step away from the premises and back into the road.

As she watched them in the mirrors, Meredith realized that she recognized many of the faces.

Jerry Winsted. Harold Coleman. Mary Beth Cooper.

All of them were snarling and red-eyed, mouths agape. She glanced back at the rifle. Even if she had enough bullets, could she really shoot these people? She didn't think so. A tear slid down her cheek.

Everything seemed so unreal. How could this have happened so fast? And how had she escaped it? Was John one of them already?

The pickup hit the pavement, entering the main road. The creatures — all of her former friends and acquaintances — were still in tow.

Meredith glued her eyes to the lone, deserted building behind her, waiting for a sign that the man she loved was still alive.

But there was nothing.

"I'm sorry, John," she whispered.

All intentions aside, she must've gotten there too late. Maybe there'd never been time at all.

A second later, just as she'd given up, she saw something in the driver's side mirror.

The door of the furniture shop had opened to a crack, exposing a bloodied hand, and a man's voice was screaming her name.

12

DAN CRASHED THE BUICK THROUGH a café window, shattering the glass and sending shards of debris over the hood of the vehicle.

"Get down!" he yelled to the two frightened girls in the backseat.

As soon as the vehicle came to a stop—the front half wedged in the store's entrance, the rear exposed on the sidewalk—he flicked on the headlights, brightening the store's interior, and opened the driver's side door.

Dan glanced over the seat behind him. Sandy and Quinn were huddled together, their lips quivering. Through the rear window he saw a flurry of hands pawing at the vehicle.

"Climb over the seat! Hurry!"

He reached out and grabbed the girls, one at a time, helping them over. Then he ushered them through the open front door and got out himself. He withdrew his pistol. Several of the creatures had made their way to the side of the vehicle, and he squeezed off a few suppressive shots, knocking them back.

"Run!" he shouted.

Sandy and Quinn took off to the back of the

store. After firing a few more rounds, he followed suit.

Dan weaved through a maze of chairs and tables, doing his best to ignore the groans and shuffles of the creatures behind him. He glued his eyes on a door in back. If they could reach it, they'd have a chance at escape.

His daughter made it to the door first. She tried the handle, and to his relief, the door swung open. She and Sandy raced into the darkness beyond.

Dan was right on their tail; a second later he was through the doorway. He slammed the door and fumbled for the lock. Without power, the room was pitch black, and he slid his hands frantically around the door's surface while bodies slammed the other side.

Finally he found a bolt at the top and slid it into place.

He turned to locate the girls, but could see nothing in the darkness.

"Quinn? Sandy?" he hissed.

He felt a hand tap his arm, and he jumped before realizing it was his daughter.

"I can't see anything, Dad. I'm scared."

The pounding on the door had increased in volume, and he could barely hear her whispered words.

"It'll be ok, honey. We just need to find the back entrance."

He took hold of her hand and led her deeper into the darkness, holding out his pistol at arms length. From the other side, he felt Sandy take hold of his arm.

He bumped something with his waist, and he grabbed onto it, determining that it was a shelf. He slid his hands along the smooth edge and followed it toward what he hoped was the back of the store.

Sweat poured down his face in droves. In the enclosed space they were in, the air was thick and humid. The stench of rotting food clogged his nostrils, and he held his breath to avoid the smell.

When they reached the end of the shelf, he struggled for balance, his feet crunching unseen objects. Finally his hand hit a wall, and he felt around it until he located the outline of a door.

He was still searching for the handle when the door behind them crashed inwards. Light flooded the room, and when he looked back, he saw a tangle of bodies plowing toward them.

"Let's go!" he shouted to the girls.

He found the handle and threw the door open.

A second later they were in the open air, the sun shining down upon them as they raced across an empty parking lot.

Quinn still clenched his hand, but Sandy had taken the lead, sprinting several steps ahead of them.

"Sandy!" he shouted. "What're you doing?"

The girl forged ahead as though she hadn't heard him, her shoes slapping the pavement. He yelled for her again. Finally she glanced back.

"Follow me!" she cried.

Dan felt Quinn's hand slipping from his fingers. Despite his attempts to pull her onward, she was having trouble keeping up. A crash erupted from behind them.

The creatures had made it outside.

He kept his eyes glued to Sandy, watching her hurdle a distant curb. Beyond it was a brick building with four metal exit doors. Dan recognized the rear entrances to a small shopping center. The girl was heading right for them.

To his surprise, rather than aiming at one of the doors, she was heading in the direction of a green metal dumpster. The top was open and folded to the side.

If the girl were to hurl herself inside, she'd immediately be trapped.

"Sandy — no!" he shouted.

Behind them, the things were narrowing the gap. Footsteps drummed the asphalt; hungry cries escaped into the air. Every few seconds Dan heard the crash of the door they'd left through, repeatedly pounding the wall as a new surge of creatures passed through it.

He had no idea how many of the things were in pursuit, but judging by the noise alone, it sounded like an army.

Sandy had reached the dumpster. Dan watched in dismay as she vaulted up the side, clung to the edge, and then pulled herself up and over.

He risked a glance over his shoulder. The road

behind them was a stampede of bodies. A few of the creatures had set their sights on the dumpster.

"Sandy! Get out of there!"

He screamed the girl's name, but she didn't respond.

Dan was starting to outpace Quinn. He could feel her lagging behind, stretching his arm like a piece of rope. For a split second he wished he could carry her, but even if they had time to pull off the maneuver, he doubted they'd move any faster.

The dumpster was only twenty feet away. He had a decision to make.

He could either go after Sandy, risking the lives of him and his daughter, or he could search for an alternate place to hide.

The rear entrances would be their best bet, but there were no door handles. From his experience, he knew they usually opened from inside.

He surveyed the remainder of the parking lot. There were two other buildings, one on either side of the building they were running toward. Both had alleyways in between. Their best bet was to slip down one of the alleys. Hopefully they could lose some of the creatures; perhaps they'd even find a better place to hide.

The thought of abandoning Sandy made him sick, but what choice did they have?

Maybe by going in the opposite direction, they could lure some of the things away from her.

Without warning, Sandy's head appeared over the top of the dumpster.

"Dan! This way!" she screamed. "I know a way in!"

At the last second Dan changed course. He veered toward the dumpster, pulling his daughter ahead of him, and lifted her up the side. Sandy was waiting at the top, and she grabbed Quinn's hands and hoisted her over. With his daughter in safely, Dan leapt up and grabbed the side, pushing with his forearms.

Fingers groped at his pant legs, and he fell slightly. The first wave of creatures had caught up, and the air behind him was filled with hisses and wails. He kicked the air, but each time he freed himself his legs hit another snag.

"Daddy! Grab my hands!"

Quinn and Sandy had stationed themselves at the top, tugging on his arms and shirt to facilitate the climb. Dan kicked the outside of the dumpster, found purchase, and pitched himself over the top.

He landed face-first in a pile of spilled garbage. The smell permeated his nose and lungs, and he coughed and spat.

"Over here!" Sandy shouted, beckoning to the other side of the dumpster.

Dan clambered to his feet. On the interior wall was a sliding plastic door, and the girl had opened it to reveal a dark hole beyond. She slid through the opening and disappeared inside.

Several of the creatures had thrown themselves

over the lip of the dumpster, and they teetered on the edge, on the verge of getting over. Dan directed his daughter in front of him, watching her vanish into the unknown, and then took the plunge himself.

No sooner had he cleared the opening than he heard the sound of a door slamming shut behind him. The moans and undulations of the things decreased in volume, and a moment later, a light flicked on, illuminating his surroundings.

Sandy stood in front of him holding a lantern. Her soft features seemed to have hardened, and for a moment he wondered if she was older than he thought. He'd originally pegged her as sixteen, now he was starting to wonder if she was in her early twenties.

By the looks of it, they'd made it inside the building and into a storeroom. The floor was covered in boxes and display racks. A single door on the other end had been boarded up; the bottom half was blocked by a desk.

He was still taking stock of his location when a banging erupted from behind him. Sandy set down the lantern and skirted over to the door they had just come through.

"Help me barricade it," she instructed.

She motioned him toward a three-shelved metal rack next to the exit. She took a stance on the floor and began to push, and Dan darted over to help. The rack groaned as they slid it over the cement and into place.

When they were finished, Sandy dusted her hands on her jeans.

"Do you think it'll hold?" Dan asked her.

"It hasn't failed me yet."

"You've been here before?"

"This is where I lived for the first few days after the infection began," she said. "I slept over there on those blankets, and I ate over there in that corner."

She pointed to each of the locations in turn, and Dan followed her gaze. Sandy's tone was calm and even, as if she were a realtor describing the newest property on the market. Gone was the frightened girl he had first seen on the rooftop; this new girl was confident and controlled.

Perhaps he'd found her at a moment of despair, and she'd since regained some of her fortitude.

Sandy walked to the corner and retrieved a set of folding chairs, then brought them to the center of the room and set them up for Dan and Quinn.

"I think the people who worked here used to use this as a break room. I found a pile of cigarette butts in one of the corners." She laughed. "I even tried smoking them once when I got bored."

Dan nodded. He stared at the chairs, but made no move to sit down. The rear entrance rattled and shook, and a chorus of fingernails scratched the exterior.

"Were there others with you?"

"No. I was alone. My parents died when I was twelve. Before all this I was living with my brother, but he didn't make it."

"Did he turn?"

"Yes."

Sandy averted her eyes, and Dan knew not to press her any further. He paced the room for a few minutes, inspecting the racks and boxes, but found nothing of any use. The door was still shaking from the efforts of the creatures.

"They'll leave when they get bored," Sandy said. "But sometimes it takes a while."

"How long did you say you were here?"

"A couple of days."

"How'd you get that dumpster in front of the door?"

"It was already there. I think someone must have sealed the place off when things first started, right after people realized what was happening. I ran into a young couple in a convenience store and they told me about it. They'd been staying here for a day or so."

"What happened to them?"

Sandy shook her head. "They didn't make it, either."

"What have you been eating?"

"When I was staying here, I would make trips into town and grab what I could find. At the lumberyard we have a stash of food."

Dan told her about the contamination, and

how, to the best of their knowledge, the food and water was the root cause of the infection. Then he told her about the provisions in the station wagon.

"We need to get that food back," he said simply. "It wouldn't be wise to trust anything else."

The girl nodded gravely.

"I still can't believe that Reginald left us behind like that. Hopefully he won't tamper with what you had in the car."

"Did you say there were ten people in the lumberyard?"

"Yes. Aside from Reginald and myself, there are eight others."

Sandy listed off the names, but Dan didn't recognize any of them. The town was small—though he knew a lot of the townsfolk, he didn't know all of them.

"Has anyone talked about leaving?" he asked.

"A few have tried, but none have returned. I think everyone else is scared. One of the survivors—Hector—came from New Mexico. He said that things are even worse there, if that's possible. They're a good group of people. Except for Reginald, of course."

Dan spoke about the agents, briefing the girl on everything they'd learned, and about the survivors they'd since parted ways with. Sandy listened intently, but didn't appear to be surprised.

"With those men in white coats shooting people, we've been trying to stay hidden. This run was the first time anyone's been out in days.

We've been taking turns when our supplies get low, but nobody's been rushing to volunteer. I was with a group of people and I got separated. That's how I ended up at the bank."

"I understand."

Dan retrieved his pistol. He examined the weapon and determined he had only two bullets remaining.

"So what's next?" Sandy asked.

Dan stared back at the door, where the cries of the creatures still rang with intensity.

"Now we wait."

13

AT THE SOUND OF JOHN'S voice, Meredith felt her heart jump in her chest. She revved the engine of the pickup and cut the wheel, turning back in the direction of the furniture shop.

She'd successfully led the creatures a few hundred feet from the building, and while she'd prefer to have them even farther away, she knew that time was not on her side. By the looks of John—or what little she'd seen of him—he appeared to be injured and in need of help.

She couldn't afford to wait any longer.

Before she knew it she was racing toward the building, the tires of the pickup kicking up dust and gravel. The creatures behind her had changed direction as well, but she'd bought herself a little time before they'd reach her. She needed to make this fast.

Meredith spun up next to the entrance and threw the vehicle into park, leaving the engine running. Then she opened the door and jumped out into the parking lot.

The door to the furniture shop stood ajar, but there was no sign of John. Her heart raced. Had he collapsed inside? Was he still waiting?

What if he'd turned?

In her haste, she'd forgotten her rifle on her seat. The only thing she'd been thinking about was rescuing him; concern for her own safety had gone out the window at the sight of him. But there was a real possibility that he'd been infected. That he could do her harm. In spite of her emotions, she needed to be cautious.

She edged up next to the door.

"John?" she called.

No answer. She kicked the door open with her foot, surveying the store's interior. Almost all the furniture had been upheaved or shattered; the remaining pieces were buttressed against the doors and windows.

She called out again.

This time she heard a murmured response. John was calling her name. She burst through the doorway, heading toward the noise.

When she caught sight of the man, her stomach tightened. John had wedged himself in a corner beneath a table, clutching his knees to his chest. His face was smeared with dirt and blood, and his left leg looked like it had been torn into. His rifle lay on the floor next to him.

"I thought you'd left," he whispered.

Meredith felt her heart swell, and she fought back the tears.

"No. I wouldn't do that."

Outside, the commotion of restless bodies had grown louder. She spun and stared out the door. The herd was overtaking the building.

"We have to move."

"I can't. My leg…"

He pointed to his jeans, which were stained and torn just below the knee.

"We have to go!"

She reached beneath the table, took hold of his hands, and pulled him to his feet. John winced in pain, and when he stood, she noticed a puddle of blood where he'd been sitting. In the time she'd known him, she'd never seen him incapacitated like this. In her head, he'd always been her rock. Strong. Indestructible.

"Oh my God, John…"

She scanned the wound she'd seen seconds earlier, noticing that it was worse than she'd thought. He'd need medical attention. In any case, they had to move.

"Come on!"

She flung his arm over her shoulder and led him to the front of the store. Several of the creatures had already reached the truck. Meredith motioned at John's rifle on the ground.

"Are there any bullets left?"

"Only two. I was saving them, in case…"

"Wait here!"

She propped him against one of the beams and darted back to retrieve it. It was a .22, similar to the model she owned, and she tucked it under her arm. John had started to sag, and she took hold of him again, saving him from falling.

Before they could take a step, one of the things

leapt through the door, fingers tearing at the air. She immediately recognized it as Scotty Maglund, a worker at the town post office. Unlike the man Meredith remembered — polite, friendly, always willing to lend a smile — the creature in front of her stared at her with a vacant expression, teeth bared and ready to gnash.

She squeezed the trigger of the rifle.

The bullet caught Kenneth in the teeth, and he sank forward, crashing into a broken chair. Next to her, John mumbled something. She pulled him forward.

"You can do it, John!"

He took several wearied steps beside her. Despite the fact that he had her outsized, she did her best to support him. She could see clearly through the door now: two of the creatures were on the bed of her pickup, flailing aimlessly at the sacks and lumber she had stored there; two others were headed right for them.

Only one bullet left Meredith.

The two things approached in succession — one behind the other. She lifted the rifle and aimed through the doorway, hoping to incapacitate them both.

Here goes nothing.

She fired her last round and struck the first in the neck. Fluid spit from the wound, and it toppled to the side, tripping up the other.

Thank God.

Meredith and John continued, reaching the

doorway, and she pulled him along to the truck just ten feet away. Once at the door, she flung it open and ushered him inside.

"Get in, John!"

She'd assumed he would need assistance, but to her surprise, he took the last few steps on his own, as if the air outside had given him a burst of energy. Once he was inside, she slammed the door and prepared to run to the driver's seat.

The creatures in the bed of the truck were already scrambling to get down. Before she could take a step, one of them leapt out at her. She tried to move, but she was too late. The thing crashed into her, and she cried out, losing her grip on the empty rifle.

Meredith pitched backward to the ground.

Her head struck the loose gravel, and she tried to roll, but the thing was already hovering over her. Unlike Scotty Maglund, this creature was one she didn't recognize. It swiped at her stomach with clawed hands, already lowering its head to feast.

She kicked and writhed, but to no avail. The thing had her pinned, and she was powerless to stop it. She opened her mouth to scream, but all her breath was gone, and the sound lodged in her throat.

Even if she got something out, there would be no one to help her. The area was covered in fields, John was on the verge of unconsciousness, and everyone she knew appeared to have turned into one of the things.

Meredith was out of luck.

The thing's eyes bore into her, two black orbs without pupils, and she batted at its cheeks. The creature's skin was soft and pliant; not what she would have expected from something so vile. At one time, the thing had been a man in his twenties. Dark hair. Chiseled features.

Now its countenance was weathered and grotesque. She gritted her teeth, thinking it was going to be the last face she saw before she died.

A gunshot rang into the air.

The top of the creature's head exploded, raining a residue of blood and bone onto her shirt and face. Before Meredith knew it, the thing had collapsed, and she pushed it off of her and rolled to safety.

When she glanced up, she saw John pointing her rifle through the open window of the pickup. He must have found it on the seat.

"Hurry!" he yelled.

She pushed herself up from the ground, her head spinning, and stumbled to the driver's side of the vehicle.

A minute later they were careening out of the parking lot.

John was more alert than he had been before,

but Meredith could tell he was in pain. His eyes fluttered, and his head sagged onto the windowsill. In spite of his condition, he looked at Meredith and smiled.

"I never would've thought you had it in you," he said.

"What's that supposed to mean?"

"I always thought you were a pacifist."

She scowled at him, but her heart warmed. It'd been so easy to hate him from a distance.

"How's your leg?" she asked.

He was still clutching his calf, which had suffered a large gash. Having cleared the furniture shop, Meredith pulled to the side of the road and threw the pickup into park. Then she dug in the seat behind her and pulled out a spare shirt she had in back.

"We're going to need to tie that up," she said.

John extended his leg, allowing her to create a makeshift tourniquet. Once she'd tied it off, she instructed him to put pressure on the wound, hoping to keep it from bleeding further.

"What happened back there?" she asked.

"I'm not sure. One minute I was making a chair for Gladys Stevens, the next minute those things were crashing through the door. I was able to fight them back for a while, and I even got them outside, but right before I closed the door one of them took a chunk out of me."

"Jesus, John."

"I'm sorry, Meredith. The last thing I wanted was to drag you into this. I put you in danger."

"I was the one who called you. And besides, I don't think there's any escaping it at this point. These things are everywhere."

She relayed her story about Sheila, Dan, and Marcy. John listened closely, his face growing more somber by the minute. Watching his reaction, she felt a renewed sense of emotion. Because everything had happened so fast, she'd barely had time to process what had occurred.

Her neighbors were dead, and they were never coming back. The thought seemed so surreal. She couldn't imagine life without them.

"Do you think anyone's left in town?" John asked.

"I'm not sure. I tried calling everyone I knew, but you were the only one that picked up."

"I can't believe—" John paused mid-sentence and grit his teeth. It looked like the pain was catching up to him. Perhaps the adrenaline rush from before had dulled some of his senses, and now that it was wearing off, the agony had returned.

"Don't speak, John. Just try to rest. I'm going to get you some help. There has to be someone in town. We can't be the only ones left."

Despite her words, Meredith felt a chill run the length of her body. Given what she'd seen on the news—how quickly infection had spread in other areas—it was quite possible they were the only ones remaining.

She swallowed and tried to focus on the road.

14

I T WAS ALMOST AN HOUR before the banging on
the storeroom door subsided. By that time
Dan's nerves were frayed. He'd been pacing
the storeroom almost the entire time with gun in
hand, waiting for the door to cave.

Luckily it had held.

In the meantime, Sandy and Quinn had spoken
in whispers, talking about school, work, and
life before the infection. Because Dan had been
keeping guard, he'd only made out bits and pieces
of the conversation.

It turned out Sandy was twenty-two years
old. Despite her youthful looks, she'd been out
of college for over a year, and she'd worked in a
local salon before the contamination hit. After her
brother had been infected and her apartment had
been breached, she'd taken to the streets, where
she'd been hiding ever since.

In light of the circumstances, Sandy managed
to keep things upbeat, and her conversation was a
much-needed distraction for Quinn.

Once the room had quieted, Sandy stood.

"Are they gone?" she asked.

Dan nodded. "I think so. Let's give it a few

minutes to be on the safe side. We don't want to go out there too soon."

Sandy joined him by the door, cocking her head to listen. Quinn had remained seated, but Dan could see her eyes fill with worry. For the last hour, it seemed she'd been able to ignore what was going on around her, comforted by her talks with Sandy. Now everything was becoming real again.

He hated to pull her from safety, but the truth was, they couldn't stay here forever. They needed to find the station wagon, and they needed to escape this town. There'd be no resting until they did. No matter how long they hid, they'd never really be safe in St. Matthews.

He'd already learned that back at the salvage yard.

Several minutes later, after hearing nothing outside, Dan tucked his pistol in his holster and grabbed hold of the shelf, and with Sandy's help, he began to move it away from the door.

As before, the shelf began to creak, and Dan winced at the noise. The last thing he wanted was for the things outside to return. When the entrance was clear, he paused again to listen.

The room was silent except for their breathing.

"Ready to go?" he asked.

The girls nodded their heads in unison. He beckoned for them to get behind him and opened the door.

The air still reeked of garbage, but it'd taken

on a new scent, mingling with the stink and sweat of the creatures. The resultant smell was nauseating. Dan covered his face with his free hand and maneuvered across the trash to the edge of the dumpster. When he'd reached the wall, he tucked the weapon in his belt and leapt up for a look across the parking lot.

All was quiet in the immediate vicinity. No sign of their pursuers.

He looked behind him, confirming that the girls had followed him.

"I'll go first," he whispered.

He hoisted his leg over the side and dropped to the pavement. In the distance he heard a scream, too high-pitched to be human.

"Come on!" he urged.

He lifted the girls over to join him. Once they were all in the lot, Dan directed the group along the wall of the building.

The transition from dark to daylight was glaring, and he squinted his eyes to see in front of him. Without the security of the storeroom to protect them, he felt naked and exposed.

When they reached the edge of the building, he stopped and poked his head around the corner. The alley was narrow and filthy, littered with papers, cans, and newspaper. At the end was a body lying facedown in a drainage puddle.

He looked both ways—behind them and in front—but saw nothing.

The three stepped through the alley. As they

progressed, he had the sudden feeling that they'd be surrounded, sandwiched in the middle by a legion of creatures. Despite his vision, nothing appeared, and they soon found themselves back on the main road. Dan took stock of their location. They were still in the downtown area, which, for St. Matthews, wasn't quite large at all.

In fact, having already traveled half the distance to the lumberyard, he figured they only had about a ten-minute walk in front of them.

Under normal circumstances that would have been a breeze, but he knew better than to think that now.

About a block later, they happened on a vehicle with the windows open. Dan ducked his head inside. The keys hung from the ignition.

The road ahead looked clear and unobstructed.

"Let's give it a try," he said. "If it starts, get in."

He opened the driver's side door and turned the key. The engine sprang to life. The girls opened the doors and got into the vehicle—Sandy in the front, Quinn in the back. Once he'd taken the driver's seat, he locked the doors and rolled up the windows.

"Do you know how to get to the lumberyard from here?" Sandy asked.

"Yes," he said. "But we'd better get moving. Those things probably heard us from a mile away."

The girls nodded.

"Buckle your seatbelts and hold on tight."

To Dan's relief, the path to the lumberyard was clear. Although there was some wreckage and rubble on the street, there was nothing he couldn't avoid. Using his knowledge of the town, he navigated some of the lesser-known thoroughfares, doing his best to avoid the rambling creatures they came across.

In a few cases, Dan had to increase speed to avoid a reaching hand or a hurtled body, but none of the creatures were able to latch onto the vehicle.

Sandy and Quinn remained silent. Unlike before, they didn't engage in any conversation; rather, they stared out the window as if intent on keeping guard of their surroundings.

Dan appreciated their vigilance, but at the same time, he was nervous.

With Sandy in the front seat, he felt the weight of another's life in his hands. How could he protect not one, but *two* others, when he could barely protect himself?

His only hope was that the lumberyard was secure, that they could get inside without issue. Reginald had stolen their vehicle, and there was a good chance he might not let them in, especially if he'd recognized Dan at the bank.

Dan would have to tread carefully.

After driving for several minutes, he slowed the vehicle, following a path of cracked pavement that led to their destination. Like the salvage yard, the lumberyard was somewhat removed from the rest of the town — the road that led to it contained only a few other abandoned commercial buildings.

He watched the surrounding structures with a nervous eye. Although the doors and windows were smashed, the interiors were covered in shadow, and he could only imagine what might be lurking inside.

His gaze drifted to the passenger beside him. Sandy was sitting upright in her seat. As they rolled further down the road, she pointed at one of the nearby buildings.

"There'll be a guard in there," she said. "Slow down."

Dan followed her gaze to a small square building on the right-hand side of the road. He recognized it as a small shipping and receiving center for a local trucking company. At one time, when the economy was better, the entire road had been booming with business. In recent years, most companies had shut down and the owners had moved on.

The receiving center — comprised of white painted plywood and several windows in front — had been boarded up, the door barricaded by a sheet of metal. In looking closer, Dan saw something he hadn't noticed before.

The black tip of a rifle was pointing through an opening in one of the windows.

He ground the car to a halt. Even if it were

another survivor, it would be best to exercise caution when approaching them. As he'd learned from Bubba in the salvage yard, the events of the last week had rattled the townspeople, and there was no predicting how anyone would react.

Especially if the person was working with Reginald.

Before he could devise a plan, Sandy jumped out of the vehicle and darted toward the building.

"Wait!" Dan shouted.

But he was too late. The girl had already covered most of the gap between the building and the car, and she waved her arms over her head, signaling the person inside.

"Charlie!" she called out.

The rifle followed her movements; for a minute Dan was sure the person was going to fire. He opened the door and poked his head out, using the cover of the vehicle to aim his pistol at the building.

"Get down, Quinn!" he yelled into the vehicle.

For several seconds, all was still.

After a brief pause, the weapon disappeared into the building. Sandy looked back at Dan.

"It's OK," she said.

A few seconds later, a man rounded the corner of the building, emerging from somewhere in back. His face was gaunt and worn, and he was wearing a black hooded sweatshirt. His dark hair was matted with sweat, and he had the beginnings of a beard. He looked to be in his mid-twenties.

He gave Sandy a quick hug, and she returned the embrace.

"I didn't think you were coming back," he said.

He propped his rifle in the dirt next to him and stared at the station wagon, where Dan was still hovering over the top. Dan had since lowered his gun, but he kept his body hidden behind the vehicle.

"Who are these folks?"

"This is Dan Lowery, and his daughter Quinn is in the car. Dan used to be a police officer," Sandy said.

"Glad to meet you, Dan," Charlie called.

Sensing that the man was harmless — or at the very least, that he wasn't going to shoot them — Dan left the cover of vehicle and walked toward him. He extended his hand and shook hands with the man.

"There are more of us up the road a ways. Do you have any idea what's going on here, officer?"

"It's a long story," Dan said. "We can tell you on the way. We were hoping to get our station wagon back."

"Reginald took their car," Sandy blurted. "And he left me in town to die."

Charlie's face furrowed.

"Why would he do that?"

"He used to be a criminal. It sounds like he —"

"Listen," Dan interjected. "We don't want any trouble. I think this may have been a misunderstanding. We just want to talk to him and sort this out. It's not safe out here. We should all get indoors."

Charlie nodded in agreement.

"Come with me," he said. "You can pull around back."

"We were hoping to get right to the lumberyard."

"Oh. Well that's fine, too. If you want I'll come with you. I'm exhausted, and Hector was supposed to take over for me an hour ago."

Dan headed back to the vehicle with Sandy and Charlie in tow. When they reached it, they got inside. Charlie propped his rifle between his knees.

"Thanks for the lift."

"No problem."

Dan switched the vehicle into drive and proceeded along the worn road. The tires bounced over rocks and sand, and he alternated his gaze between the rearview mirror and the road ahead, ensuring that their course was safe.

"So you're a police officer?" Charlie asked, his brow raising.

"Yes. At least I was, before all of this happened. I was one of only four in town, but the others didn't make it."

Dan studied the man beside him. If he was from St. Matthews, he didn't recognize him.

"Where you from, Charlie?"

"I'm from Texas. I was out here on a road trip with two of my friends, and we got sidetracked when the shit hit the fan. Some men on I-40 started shooting at us. I was the only one that got away."

Charlie's eyes grew wide, and he turned his attention out the window. Dan wondered how many times he'd told his story, whether it ever got any easier. He suspected it didn't.

"Sandy says there are ten of you at the lumberyard?"

"Yea. Reginald, Sandy, myself, and seven others. There used to be more of us, but a few people decided to leave and never came back."

"Did you all know each other before this?"

"No. Most of us met up in town, in the midst of all this shit. It was Reginald's idea to come here. Ever since we arrived, we've been taking turns at the guard station and running into town for supplies."

Dan nodded. They were almost at the lumberyard; he could see the closed gates from here.

"Will somebody be here to let us in?"

"There should be. We've been taking turns keeping watch. We had a few close calls with the things almost getting over the fence, which is why we set up the extra perimeter at the guard shack. It gives us a little extra time to prepare."

"Got it."

Dan slowed the vehicle to a stop about ten feet from the entrance. Beyond the chain-link fence he saw several buildings: a main warehouse, a small red building that looked like an office, and a repository for lumber that was stored outside. The place looked deserted.

"Are you sure anybody's home?" Dan asked.

He looked behind him and noticed that Sandy and Charlie were both looking toward the small red building on the other side of the fence. He followed their stare, but saw nothing of interest. The small structure had only one door facing the gate; it was closed.

"Usually somebody's inside. I think it was Tom's turn to watch," Charlie said. He frowned. "We don't usually leave the entrance unmanned. I'll go and rattle the gate to get their attention. Wait here."

Dan watched as the young man exited the vehicle, leaving his rifle in the car. He stalked over to the fence, scanning in all directions, and then clasped his fingers around it and started to shake.

"Tom? You in there?"

Charlie pressed his face against the metal, peering into the yard. After a minute, Dan saw movement from the red building: the door cracked and a face peeped out.

Without warning, the door swung open and the person inside started to shoot. Sandy screamed out for them to stop, but she was too late.

The bullets had found their mark, and Charlie pitched backward and collapsed in the dirt.

15

T HE TOWN CENTER WAS ONLY a few minutes away. As she drove, Meredith kept a close watch on John, suddenly fearful that he would lose consciousness.

If he passed out, how would she revive him? What if there was no help to be found?

Since leaving the furniture shop, she'd seen no signs of life on the roadway, no evidence that others had survived. The quiet in the air was all encompassing. Instead of giving her relief, it gave her unease.

"Stay with me, John," she said.

Her companion had slumped over further in the seat, his head pressed against the windowsill. It looked like his leg had started bleeding again. She reached over and shook his shoulder, and he blinked to attention.

"Sorry. I'm trying to stay awake," he said.

In the horizon, Meredith could make out specks of buildings growing closer. It was the first inkling of town she'd seen since everything started happening, and she felt a sense of dread creep through her body.

Normally the town gave her a sense of comfort, but not today.

Minutes later she was passing the first signs of civilization. She hit the brakes, inspecting each structure. On the surface, the buildings seemed normal enough. The houses and shops were all as she remembered them: quaint, familiar, and inviting. Aside from the lack of people, it might as well have been another day in town, and she could very well have been on one of her grocery runs or taking a trip to the store.

It was when she looked closer that the subtle differences started to reveal themselves.

Doors had been left open; windows were ajar. Although the town was small and trusting, things seemed different than usual, as if an aura of foreboding had descended over the buildings.

About a block into town she noticed a shadow in one of the windows, and she hit the brakes and slowed to a stop. The figure was in motion, roving from one room to the next. Although she was unable to make out the person's details, she knew whom the house belonged to. The owner's name was Deborah Fratzel.

Meredith cranked down the window and called out toward the building.

"Deb? You in there?"

The figure became more animated, roaming even faster. Like many of the other properties, the entrance to Deborah's house was open; Meredith could make out the woman's living room through the front door.

"Hello?"

The figure was at a window adjacent to the living room, on the right-hand side of the house. Before Meredith knew it, the figure was on the move. The person crashed through the living room and out into the open, descending down the front set of steps and toward the pickup.

It was Deborah, but her hair was wild, her fingernails poised and feral. Her face was covered in blood, as if she'd dipped herself in a vat of the crimson fluid. Meredith flashed back to the scene she'd witnessed earlier—the one with Sheila and Marcy—and shuddered.

She hammered the gas pedal with her foot, tires spinning, and tore off down the road. In the mirrors she saw Deborah chasing behind them.

As they progressed deeper into town, more shadows appeared in the windows, but she knew better than to stop. All of their movements were erratic, their gestures inhuman.

With the streets barren, Meredith was suddenly conscious of the noise she was making. The town had fallen into relative silence—no machinery running, no chatter of conversation—and the pickup's engine seemed exponentially louder, echoing off the surrounding buildings like an air horn.

Before long, the shadows around her had emerged onto the street. The creatures had picked up on the noise, and they barreled out of the surrounding entrances with alarming speed.

Meredith recognized many of their faces, but

instead of welcoming grins, their mouths had drawn up into possessed sneers. She pushed the truck faster, tumbling through the streets in a haze.

Everything she'd known was gone.

She opened her mouth to speak, but the words came out in little more than a whisper.

"We shouldn't have come here."

She looked next to her for John's reaction, but his eyes had closed and his hands had collapsed to his sides. She listened frantically for a sign that he was breathing, but heard none.

All she could hear was the roar of the pickup's engine as the vehicle drove deeper into a town that felt like hell.

Several streets later, having outrun her pursuers, Meredith took a left-hand turn into a parking lot with two small office buildings. Both were brick and square; each held a sign out front. The one on the left belonged to Dr. Steadman.

She needed to get John help, and fast.

Her only hope was that somehow the doctor had escaped the infection, that maybe he was somewhere inside. The nearest hospital was towns away.

The parking lot contained several vehicles, but none were occupied. Meredith backed into the handicapped space right next to the door and threw off her seatbelt. She leaned over and touched John's neck, searching for a pulse.

It was faint, but there.

This time when she listened close, she heard the wisp of his breath, and she could see that his chest was rising and falling. In any case, he wasn't out of the water yet. He'd lost a lot of blood, and he needed stitches and his wound cleaned. Although Meredith wasn't a doctor, she knew that much.

Given John's size, there was no way she could carry him. She'd have to go in alone. Meredith unlocked the door and grabbed the rifle, then jumped into the parking lot.

She gave one last look around. The parking lot was empty. Relieved, she slammed the door shut and dashed up to the entrance, leaving the vehicle running.

The doorway contained a covered overhang and two doors — one to a dental office, the other to Dr. Steadman's. She tried both handles, but both were locked. She banged on the door to the doctor's office.

"Dr. Steadman? It's Meredith Tilly! I need help!"

There was a window on the right side of the doorway, and she leaned off the steps to get a look inside. What she saw made her heart drop. The waiting room had been torn apart: magazines littered across the floor, chairs overturned, supplies scattered. The glass window leading to the reception area was smashed.

There was no sign of Dr. Steadman or his employees.

Undeterred, she rapped on the windowpane, screaming the doctor's name once again. At the same time, she kept a watch on the parking lot, certain that she'd draw the attention of some of the infected nearby.

It was a risk she had to take. John needed treatment. She couldn't fail him.

In spite of her efforts, there was no response.

She kicked the door below the handle, hoping to cave it in inwards, but it held fast. She was just about to try the back of the building when a pale white face appeared at the window. Meredith jumped back.

She instantly recognized Dr. Steadman: round, bespectacled, and sporting a thin gray moustache. The man's mouth hung agape, and he stared at her with vacant eyes. In spite of his appearance, he didn't seem to be infected. She waved her arms, hoping to snap him out of the trance he was in, and motioned to the door.

"Let me in!" she shouted.

The man at the window stared at her but didn't move. She continued to yell, banging on the pane in front of him. After a few seconds he disappeared from sight.

She waited another minute, but the door remained closed.

Footsteps rang out behind her. Meredith spun.

Across the street, one of the building doors had

crashed open and a mound of creatures spilled from inside. Her breath caught in her throat, her instincts screaming at her to run. She stared at the back of the pickup, where John's motionless figure sat inside. She turned back to the window.

"Help!" she screamed.

She pounded the door again, then she raised her foot to kick it. Before she could exact the maneuver, the door swung open and someone tugged her inside, slamming the door shut behind her.

Meredith was in the waiting room. The doctor stood in front of her, hands shaking.

"Meredith?" he asked, as if she might somehow transform into someone else.

"Yes, it's me."

"My God."

The doctor reached out and took hold of her sleeve, pinching the fabric as if to verify she was real. In all her dealings with the man, he'd always been stoic and professional. She'd never seen him lose his calm, and she'd never seen him rattled. Now, as he looked her up and down, it looked like he'd encountered a ghost.

"Dr. Steadman, I need your help. John Parish is injured, and he—"

Thud-thud-thud.

Before she could finish her thought, the door shook behind them, straining against the hinges. Dr. Steadman fell against it, shielding the entrance with his body. Inhuman cries spilled from the other side, and he cried out with each blow, holding his forehead with his hands as if to will the creatures away.

Meredith raced to the window and stole a glance. The creatures had bombarded the front steps; a few were lingering around the pickup. By the looks of it, John still hadn't moved.

I shouldn't have left him behind.

But what else could she have done? John needed medical treatment, and she'd found him a doctor. What she couldn't have anticipated was that the doctor would be in such a frayed emotional state.

She glanced over at Dr. Steadman, who'd tucked himself into a ball by the door. His eyes met hers, and he shook his head, as if hoping to clear the images that resided there.

In order to get his help, she'd have to snap him out of it.

"Doc! Help me secure the door!"

She grabbed his arm and led him to a coffee table in the center of the room, then instructed him to help her carry it. The two hoisted it in front of the door. Once the table was in place, Meredith snagged several of the waiting room chairs and propped them above the table. It wasn't the best barricade, but it would have to do.

"Is there anyone else in the building?" she asked.

"N-no," the doctor stammered. "Everyone left when this all started happening. I watched them leave the parking lot, but then some of them came back when they turned into those things. In fact, I think that's Rosa — my nurse — right outside."

Meredith listened as a high-pitched shriek erupted from beyond the door.

"We need to get your medical supplies and get to John Parish. He's in the truck, and he needs our help. This is an emergency."

The doctor nodded and tipped his glasses back on his nose.

"What happened?"

"He was bitten by one of them and there's a huge gash in his leg. He's lost a lot of blood, and he's been in and out of consciousness."

She watched the doctor's demeanor change, his expression harden. It was as if the prospect of treating John had somehow jolted him back into reality. Her only hope was to keep him focused.

"We need to hurry!"

"Let's go back to my office and grab some things," he said. "After that, we can find a way out of here."

16

CHARLIE TWITCHED ON THE GROUND and then grew still. His hooded sweatshirt had been ripped apart by bullets, his stomach covered in blood. The figure in the red shack ducked back inside and out of sight. It sounded like he'd run out of bullets. At the same time, it was very possible that he had another weapon.

Dan held his position behind the door of the Buick.

At the sound of gunfire, he'd instructed the girls to stay down in the backseat. He peered behind him to make sure they were all right. Sandy's face was wet with tears; her lips trembled.

"Who's in the shack?" he asked.

"It looks like Reginald. But why would he do this? I don't understand."

"Maybe he knows we're here for the car. Maybe he's found what we have inside, and he's putting the pieces together. Whatever the case may be, we need to get inside, and we need to get that food."

"I'll talk to him. This must be a misunderstanding. He must've mistaken Charlie for—"

"I wouldn't trust him, Sandy. I know this man. The way things are right now, there's a good chance he'll shoot you the way he did to Charlie. You'd better stay put and let me handle this."

Dan turned his attention back to the front gate. The lumberyard was graveyard silent. Nothing moved, nothing in sight. Still, he could sense that the man was lurking within the building, maybe even waiting to line up another shot.

He'd already killed one of his comrades. It would be foolish to think he wouldn't kill anyone else if he had the means. Dan lowered the window to a crack and yelled out of the opening.

"Reginald? I know you're in there. This is Dan Lowery with the St. Matthews Police Department."

The yard was silent.

"I'm not here to arrest you, but you have something of ours that we need back. Give us the car and we'll be on our way."

A few seconds of silence passed. Finally, a response rang through the yard.

"Bullshit."

Dan tensed at the word, but did his best to remain cool.

"I'm telling the truth," he called out.

"I know exactly what you're looking for, you pig cocksucker. I've seen what you have in the car." Reginald paused. "And there's no way I'm giving it up. You think I want to die like everybody else?"

"Throw all of your weapons and open the gates. We'll talk about it."

Laughter filled the lumberyard, echoing off

the gates and drifting out to the car. Dan bit his lip. He needed another opening, an advantage.

"I have my daughter with me, Reginald. She's only eleven years old. I'm not looking for trouble. I just want our vehicle and our things."

"Not happening. The food is ours now."

"How long do you think that food will last you, anyway? A few weeks at most? I can tell you where to get more."

"If you don't need it, then why did you come here?"

"Because there are things in that car that I can't replace. Open up, Reginald."

There was a long pause. Dan looked back at the girls. Both of them were staring at him intently, their eyes round and hopeful.

When he glanced back over the dash, he saw a figure emerge from the shack and throw a weapon in the dirt. It was Reginald, and he was dressed in the same attire they'd seen him in hours earlier: a black jean jacket, dark jeans, and boots. He'd left his gun in the dirt by the shack.

When he reached the fence, he fiddled with a padlock in the center, then hung it on one of the links and swung open the gates.

"All right. Come on in inside," he said. "Maybe we can make a deal."

The man stood about twenty feet from the car with his arms raised. Charlie's lifeless body lay on the ground next to him.

"Stay put," Dan told the girls.

In spite of the man's words, he still didn't trust him. It was possible Reginald had another weapon on him.

Dan rolled the driver's side window back up and felt for the door handle. Then he opened the door and propped his gun through the crack.

"Keep your hands in the air," he called out.

Reginald remained in place, obedient. Dan swung his feet onto the asphalt and slowly exited the vehicle, keeping his pistol trained in front of him. As he advanced, he heard the man chuckling.

"What's so funny?" Dan asked.

"It's just ironic. Even at the end of the world, some things never change."

"What's that supposed to mean?"

"Doesn't this feel like déjà vu, Officer Lowery? This isn't the first time we've been in this situation, you and I. We've got a lot of history together."

"All I'm looking for is my car."

"How many times have we done this dance? Three?"

"I don't remember."

"Sure you do. You were the one responsible for sending me to prison for the first time. Back in 2008."

"I was just doing my job."

"And I appreciate it. I learned a lot while I was locked up, and I have you to thank for it. In a lot of ways, you're the reason I'm still alive."

Dan's eyes wandered to Charlie's body, and he shook his head. Had the man lost his mind?

"You're delusional, Reginald."

"No, I'm not. But I'm a lot smarter now that I was then."

Without another word, Reginald whistled into the air. Dan furrowed his brow, still unsure of the man's intentions.

A second later he understood.

Three men with guns had appeared from behind the red shack. They crept through the dirt, advancing toward the fence, and trained their rifles at Dan and the vehicle.

Reginald turned and smiled. "Got you this time, pig."

Dan lay facedown in the shack, his mouth tasting dirt and grime. He'd been stripped of his weapon, and his hands and feet were bound. The girls were tied up next to him.

Quinn was whimpering. She'd originally been screaming, but the men had placed a gag in her mouth to silence her. The sound of his daughter struggling made him sick to his stomach.

"It's OK, honey," he said, his words shaky and uncertain.

For the last ten minutes he'd been struggling with his bindings, attempting to wriggle free, but the ropes had held firm. Dan was hopelessly contained.

The shack that they were being kept in was

small — no more than fifteen feet wide and fifteen feet across. The walls were made of natural oak; the interior was little more than a frame. Aside from the three of them, there was nothing else in the room that Dan could see, nothing that could offer them assistance.

He turned to his left to face Sandy. Her face was streaked with tears. Even though she'd begged and protested, her former comrades had insisted on tying her up, insisting that she could no longer be trusted.

"Any idea where they went?"

She shook her head.

On the way in, Dan had gotten a better view of the lumberyard. Just past the guard shack was a large warehouse where most of the lumber was stored, beyond it a rectangular structure with gray vinyl siding. He assumed the group was holing up in the latter building.

Even though Reginald had kept them alive, Dan was hesitant to believe they'd be kept that way. After what Reginald had done to Charlie, it was obvious he'd snapped.

The only thing he needed Dan for now was information.

Dan opened his mouth to ask Sandy another question, but before he could, footsteps sounded from outside. The men were returning. He turned his head away from Sandy and focused at the wall in front of him. The men hadn't injured them yet.

The last thing he needed was to give them an excuse.

There were three voices in earshot, and Dan instantly recognized one of them as Reginald's.

"We'll keep them in there until we get what we want."

"I don't like this one bit, Reginald. Why don't we just send them on their way?"

"The cop has information that can keep us safe."

"What if somebody's looking for him?"

"We're in the middle of a goddamn apocalypse. Don't worry about it."

The voices hushed as the footsteps grew closer. Dan heard the creak of a door, and then the three men were inside with them. He kept his eyes glued to the wall. A second later he felt a sharp pain in his side; someone had kicked his ribs. The blow knocked the wind out of him, and he coughed and spat on the floor.

He heard the floorboards creak, and then he saw the bridge of Reginald's nose as he leaned down beside him.

"How's it going down there, Dan? It doesn't feel so good when the shoe's on the other foot, does it?"

The other men in the room chuckled. Dan craned his neck, but could make out only several blurry figures. His gaze wandered back to Reginald. The man sneered at him, eyes dark and penetrating.

"I've told the group all about you. It's obvious you have something to do with this—the food in your car proves it. Everyone agreed that we should do what's necessary to protect ourselves."

"I have nothing to do with the infection, Reginald."

"Funny, that's not what you said before."

The other men in the room murmured.

"What are you talking about?"

Reginald continued.

"I know you're behind this. You're going to tell us how to survive this thing, and I'm going to take every measure I can to get you to talk."

"I have nothing to do with this. I'm a goddamn police officer, for Christ's sake. Do these men know about your past, Reginald? Do they know what kind of man you are? You just killed one of your own in cold blood!"

He strained his head again, wishing he could make eye contact with the men behind him. He tried rolling over, but Reginald held him down.

"We've all made mistakes. I've told these men that. Shooting Charlie was an accident. I saw a strange car and a hooded man at the gate that I didn't recognize. I acted on instinct. I feel bad about what happened, but all I can do is move forward."

"You knew exactly who he was. You're a goddamn murderer."

"And what does that make you, Dan? You're responsible for the deaths of thousands of people, and you're putting our entire group in danger by being here. You're going to tell us what we need to know, and then we're going to make sure that you can't hurt anyone else."

Quinn cried out, but her words died in the gag. Dan looked over at her. His heart was pounding, and he was fighting from welling up.

"I'm going to make you a deal, Dan. You tell us what we need to know — *everything* — and we'll let your daughter live."

Clearly the man was manipulating the situation, and he'd convinced his comrades that Dan was a threat.

Dan kept his eyes locked on his daughter's, refusing to look at the man. After everything that they'd been through, everything they'd survived, he couldn't help but feel that this was the end of the line.

With his hands and feet bound, there was nothing he could do to save himself, no action he could take to remedy the situation. All he could do was to try and save his daughter.

Reginald glared at him, still waiting for an answer. Finally Dan responded.

"Deal."

17

DR. STEADMAN DASHED BETWEEN THE examination rooms, Meredith on his heels. Despite putting some distance between themselves and the front entrance, Meredith could still hear the incessant pounding of hands on the wood, and the sounds kept her nerves on edge.

The doctor began to hand her equipment, and she took it with open arms, glad she'd been able to spur him into action. After searching through several drawers and cabinets, the man pulled out a black leather bag and handed it to her.

"Dump everything in here," he said.

She complied, filling the bag with the sutures, needles, and bandages. When the bag was full, the doctor took it from her and slung it over his arm.

"We need to get out of here. There's an entrance on the side of the building; hopefully we can sneak outside. Provided those things haven't surrounded the building, of course."

Meredith nodded. Before proceeding, the doctor looked her in the eye.

"I was afraid, Meredith. I thought I was the only one left. I'm so glad you showed up."

"Me too."

"Thank you for coming; I'm not sure what I would've done otherwise."

"You're welcome."

"Now let's get out of here. We need to get to John. Depending on how much blood he's lost, he might be in trouble. Follow me."

Meredith retrieved the rifle from the ground and followed him as he made his way out of the examination room. The doctor led her down a back hallway, then into a supply room filled with prescription samples and equipment. She'd been in the office several times, but never back this far.

At the other end of the room was a door with several latches. It looked like it hadn't been used in a while. The doctor groped at a metal chain at the top, preparing to slide it out of the lock.

"Ready?" he asked.

She swallowed and held up the rifle. "Yep. I'll lead the way."

"I'm going to leave it open a few inches—that way if things get bad we'll have a way back in."

Meredith nodded. The doctor unlocked the door and swung it open. A wide sliver of daylight crept through the crack, illuminating the floor. Before she knew it, Meredith was outside, her feet pounding the pavement.

The closest building was about fifty feet away, buffered by a row of neatly trimmed hedges. In front of her was a paved parking lot leading to the front. The creatures had started to trickle around the building toward them. She hoisted her gun under her arm, mentally counting the bullets. If she recalled correctly, there were only a few rounds left.

Once the bullets were gone, things would get even worse.

The doctor ran behind her, his breath coming in spurts. Several times she glanced back, certain that he'd be yanked away by one of the creatures, but each time he was still there, unharmed.

Within seconds they'd covered the ground between the side of the building and the front — about twenty feet or so, and they were approaching the edge of the wall. Meredith could see the tail end of the pickup, and she felt her heart pounding in her chest.

Had the things gotten to John?

She'd locked the doors and closed the windows before exiting, and he'd barely been conscious. Were the creatures attracted to movement? If so, there was a good chance he was safe; at the same time, everything about the infected was unknown.

If something happened to him she'd never forgive herself.

"Meredith! Watch out!"

One of the creatures careened toward her. She felt for the trigger of the rifle, but at the last second, she decided better of it.

She needed to preserve her ammunition.

Meredith rotated the rifle in her hands and swung it like a bat. Her weapon connected with the thing's head, sending it reeling to the pavement.

Before she could catch her breath, another had taken its place. She reared the rifle back for another blow and swung, catching it with the wooden stock.

The doctor had paused behind her, and she spun to ensure he was uninjured. He gave her a hurried nod to proceed.

A few steps later the truck was in full view. To Meredith's relief, the bulk of the creatures had congregated at the office doors, and though a few were lurking near the pickup, none had found their way inside. John's slumped figure remained in the passenger's seat, oblivious to the chaos around him.

"Hurry, doc!" she cried.

Having taken care of the two closest creatures, Meredith had created an opening to the truck. If they ran fast enough, there was a chance they'd make it to the pickup without another encounter.

She increased her speed. They'd almost reached the bed of the truck when she heard the man behind her falter. She spun in time to see his legs go out from under him and his face crack the pavement. His glasses burst on his face, scattering shards on the ground around him. He'd lost the bag he was carrying, and it skittered to a stop next to Meredith's feet.

"Get up!" she shrieked.

The doctor groaned, but his cries were quickly drowned out by the moans of the creatures.

When Meredith looked left, she saw that the

swarm at the front door had broken formation. One by one the things were plowing toward the doctor. It was as if they'd been waiting for the right moment to strike, and they'd chosen this exact moment to do so.

Meredith lunged for the man's arm, hoping to pull him up, but one of the things had already reached his lower half, and it tugged on his legs and pulled him out of her grasp. She raised her rifle and fired a round. The bullet found its mark, but she was too late — others had already flooded the scene; within seconds the doctor was overwhelmed.

The man screamed in agony as his body was torn apart, blood oozing from tears and lacerations in his midsection. Meredith bit back her tears and cast a look back at the truck.

There was nothing she could do to help the man, but John still needed her. And if she were to give up now, everything she'd done would have been in vain.

The leather bag sat at her feet. She snagged it from the ground, swung it over her shoulder, and weaved around several of the lunging creatures, working her way toward the truck.

When she reached it, she flung open the door and jumped inside.

As she backed the pickup out of the parking lot, a landscape now filled with the infected, she tried to locate the body of Dr. Steadman. The place where he'd fallen was covered in moving limbs, his body swallowed whole in the wake of the creatures.

It was as if he'd never existed at all.

"Where are we?" John asked.

He blinked his eyes slowly at Meredith, as if he were seeing her for the first time. All around them were numbered wooden posts, with grass creeping up to fill the spaces between. Directly in front of the pickup was a gigantic rectangular screen. The sides were curled and cracked, the surface marred with age.

"We're at the drive in," Meredith said.

John wrinkled his brow, confused. Given what he'd just been through, Meredith was glad to see him awake. It was no wonder that he couldn't remember.

In Meredith's hands was the black leather bag from the doctor's office. The contents were spread over her lap, and her gloved fingers were still covered in John's blood. She'd never stitched a wound before, but she *did* know how to sew, and after looking over the contents of the doctor's bag, she'd done her best to clean and suture the wound.

A few minutes into the procedure John had passed out from the pain. Now, fifteen minutes after she'd finished, he'd regained consciousness.

She slipped off the rubber gloves and tossed

them out the open window. Then she set the bag down on the floor below her and reached for his hand. He took it, locking her fingers into his.

"I can't believe you just did that," he said, inspecting the bandage on his leg.

"Me neither. I just hope it holds. How are you feeling?"

She could see that John was wincing.

"I've been better," he admitted, fiddling with the bandage on his leg.

"Leave it alone. It'll need time to heal."

Although she wasn't a doctor, Meredith was impressed by the job she'd done. At the same time, she wanted to have John inspected by a professional. That was the only way to ensure he'd been treated properly.

Still, the bleeding had stopped and John was alive. And for that she was grateful.

She gazed up at the screen, recalling the many times she'd been here during childhood. The drive-in had been closed for almost fifteen years, but she'd had plenty of good memories here. At one time, the Settler's Creek Theater had been the largest attraction for miles, drawing in crowds from all the neighboring towns.

Now the area was overgrown, lifeless.

She let her eyes wander to the sky. In the time they'd been there, dusk had settled over the field and the stars had started to emerge. She followed the spatter of lights, her eyes settling on the largest. As a child, she'd always had an interest in astronomy, and she recognized it as the North Star. Regardless of how the earth was spinning, it was the one light in the sky that never seemed to move.

Despite the horrors that were happening to the world below it, the star remained untouched. The sight of it gave her a feeling of warmth that she hadn't felt in a while.

"I've never been to the drive-in," John said. "Can you believe that?"

"You have now."

Meredith smiled at him, squeezing his hand.

"I'm not sure this qualifies," he said. "Something's missing."

"Popcorn?"

"That must be it."

"I thought you were going to ask where the movie was."

"I don't need a movie, Meredith," he said. "All I need is you."

John leaned over, still grimacing, and kissed her on the lips.

"I missed you, Meredith."

She smiled. Although circumstances had uncovered buried feelings, she couldn't forget the hurt that John had put her though.

But there would be time for that later. Or so she hoped.

"I missed you too," she said.

The two gazed up into the sky, and for the next few minutes, the rest of the world was forgotten.

18

"THE PEOPLE RESPONSIBLE CALL THEMSELVES the agents," Dan said.

The three men sat in front of him in wooden chairs, their eyes glued to his, all giving their undivided attention. Although it was unclear whether they believed him, it was obvious that Dan had captured their attention. The men listened without a word as he recounted his story.

He spoke of the attack by his former partner Howard, the raid at the salvage yard, and the information they'd gleaned from the fallen agent. He also told them about how he thought they might be immune, though he couldn't be sure.

While he was talking, Dan took the opportunity to size up his captors. Aside from Reginald, it was the first time he'd gotten a look at the others, and he noted that the other two men were considerably larger than the first.

The man to Reginald's left was bald and heavyset, wearing a simple blue button-up shirt, jeans, and a pair of work boots. Dan pegged him as a tradesman of some sort, perhaps a construction worker. The man to Reginald's right was tall and rugged, with toned arms, dark hair, and a sleeve of tattoos. His eyes were dark and brooding, and he pierced Dan with his stare.

The girls had been left in the shack, and Dan had been taken alone to a far corner of the lumberyard, in a small building with a cement floor and a high ceiling. He hadn't noticed the building before, but when he saw it, he had a sinking feeling that it might be his final resting place.

On the way over, he'd glimpsed the warehouse and the main buildings, and he'd seen several faces peeking out at him from dust-covered windows. Although he was unable to discern any of their features, he thought he noticed several women, perhaps even a young child.

He could only imagine what Reginald had told them. At the very least, they must have been instructed to stay indoors.

Throughout the conversation, Dan had been struggling with his bonds, but so far he'd been unable to loosen them. He'd been propped up on a chair, and the men were between him and the single exit. When he finished speaking, he sucked in a breath, waiting for whatever was to happen next.

The men exchanged glances, as if they were suddenly unsure. After a long pause, the bald man on the left opened his mouth to speak.

"I believe him."

Reginald shifted his gaze to the other man. The man with the tattoos pulled at his chin and his eyes fell to the ground.

"I do, too."

Reginald's face grew dark. Without warning, he flew up from his chair, knocking it over.

"This man is a fucking liar!" he yelled, pointing his finger in Dan's face. "You believe all that shit he's telling you? He's part of it! He's the one who did this!"

The other men remained silent, eyes averted.

"If you aren't going to take care of him, I will!"

Reginald pulled out a pistol and leveled it at Dan's head.

"Any last words, you piece of shit?"

"Promise me that my daughter will be safe," Dan said.

Reginald's face remained tense, angry. Instead of responding, he moved several inches closer to his target.

Before he could pull the trigger, the tattooed man stood abruptly. Reginald looked back, startled.

"This isn't right, Reginald. He's a goddamn cop, for fuck's sake. If you're going to do this, I don't want any part in it."

"Me neither," the bald man said, taking to his feet.

Reginald's face fell, and he lowered the gun.

"Where are you going?" he asked them.

The men ignored him. Reginald took a step toward them, but they'd already exited the room, and the door slapped closed behind them. Dan heard their footsteps scuff the dirt as they walked across the lot. A few seconds later, the noises faded and Reginald turned back to face him.

"I guess it's just me and you, officer shit bag."

"I wouldn't do this if I were you," Dan said. "You know that I'm telling the truth, and your friends do, too. If you do this you'll drive a wedge between the group, and that's the last thing you need at a time like this."

Reginald glared at him with disgust.

"Talk it over first. Make sure everyone is in agreement before you pull that trigger."

"I don't give a shit what anyone else thinks. I don't answer to anyone but myself."

The man raised the pistol to Dan's forehead again, gritting his teeth. Beads of perspiration dotted his forehead, and his hand shook. Dan closed his eyes and steeled himself on the chair, waiting for the bullet that would signify the end.

Seconds passed. He heard the other man breathing, heard his own breath accelerate. He strained at the ropes, giving one last-ditch effort to break free, but his hands and feet wouldn't move. At any second he was sure that a wave of pain would wash over him.

Goodbye, Quinn.

Only the gunshot never came.

When Dan opened his eyes he saw that Reginald had tucked the gun in his pants. The man was shaking his head.

"Don't get comfortable, pig," he said. "I'll be

right back as soon as I talk to the others. I doubt it'll take long."

Without another word, he stalked off through the door and into the cool desert night, taking the lantern with him.

Dan strained in the dark for what felt like hours, until his wrists and ankles were raw from the rope. The chair he was in had been lashed to a single beam in the room—no matter how hard he tried, he was unable to tip it.

As he fought to break free, he thought of his daughter. Was she still in the same place, and was she safe?

He'd been listening for signs of her from outside, but hadn't heard anything that resembled Quinn. Every so often he heard the patter of shoes, but each time, no voices accompanied them. He imagined that it was the switching of guards at the shack, perhaps someone keeping watch over the yard.

At some point soon they'd come for him. And next time he wouldn't be so lucky.

Though he'd been able to convince Reginald to keep him alive, at least for the moment, he had little faith that the man would release him. It was obvious the man had a personal vendetta against him.

And what better time to exact revenge than when the world was ending?

His only hope was that the rest of the group would object to his treatment. Perhaps that would buy him more time.

He needed to get out of here, and he needed to help Quinn.

Heart pounding, he pitched himself forward in the chair, but to no avail. A few minutes later he heard a noise from outside the building. Dan stopped writhing and stood still, listening.

The noise was faint at first: it sounded like it was coming from somewhere across the yard. He heard the creak of a door, then the sound of footfalls crunching the dirt.

It sounded like someone was coming his way.

Dan tensed.

He tugged against the ropes with all his might, pain creeping up his arms. The footsteps drew closer, and then, abruptly, they stopped.

It sounded like the person was right outside the door.

Although he couldn't see anything, he could sense someone's presence, and when he listened hard enough, he could hear the person breathing. Dan went stock-still. Whoever the person was must be aware that he was in here.

Why hadn't they announced themselves?

He was tied up, after all. What harm could he possibly do them?

The door cracked open, and a thin patch of

moonlight appeared on the floor. A second later a shadow slipped inside. The door clicked shut.

Dan's forehead dripped with sweat. He heard a footstep. Then another. The person was right in front of him. A whispered voice broke the silence.

"Stay quiet."

All of a sudden a pale light flicked on, and he saw the frightened visage of Sandy in front of him. In her hands was a knife. She reached toward him, and for a split second, Dan feared she was going to stab him.

Instead, she sawed at the ropes on his legs, fraying the fibers and breaking him free. When she was finished, she cut loose his hands.

Dan stood, shaking out the stiffness that had set into his limbs. The circulation slowly returned to his legs, and he had to fight from falling. Sandy was staring at him.

"Get out of here," she hissed.

He looked at her in surprise.

"How'd you get in here? How'd you escape?"

"The others set me free, but Reginald isn't happy. Everyone's arguing, and it's not looking good for you."

"Where's my daughter?"

"I already broke her loose. You need to get out of here, Dan, and never look back."

Sandy reached over to hand him something. He saw that it was a set of keys. When he looked down at them, he instantly recognized the keychain. They were *his* — one of them belonged to the stolen station wagon.

"Quinn's already inside. Follow me and keep as low as possible. We don't want to alert the guard."

"Didn't they see you coming over here?"

"I slipped out while they were arguing. Come on, there's no time to explain."

"Aren't you coming?"

She hesitated. "No. I can't. People need me here. I can't leave them behind."

Before Dan knew it the girl was treading across the floor and opening the door. He followed behind her, his limbs still aching from his restraints. When he slipped out into the night, the cool air soothed his skin, and he drew a silent breath as he hunkered down behind her.

Sandy led him over to the fence, away from the main building, and behind the warehouse. Dan did his best to pad his footsteps, knowing that one wrong move could alert the others. Sandy was taking a huge risk by helping him — surely the others would figure out what she'd done, and she'd have to explain herself.

In any case, he was grateful.

He kept low to the ground as he ran. Soon they'd made it behind the building. By the light of the moon, he could see several shapes behind the lot, and recognized one of them as the station wagon.

When he got close, he saw a shadow in the backseat. *Quinn.*

His heart flooded with relief, and he cracked the driver's door and slipped inside. His daughter lunged for his shoulders, and he clung to her for a second before locating the key.

"Daddy," she whispered, crying.

"It's ok," he responded. "Everything will be all right."

Sandy remained outside the vehicle. She crouched beside the driver's side door, whispering instructions.

"They'll be looking for me soon. I have to leave. I think you should be able to drive through the gate. From what I've seen, it's not the sturdiest."

"Why don't you come with us?"

"I need to make sure the others are safe. Everyone needs to know about Reginald before it's too late."

"Won't you be in danger?"

"I'll be fine. It's a risk I have to take."

Dan reached out and took the girl's hand.

"Thank you, Sandy."

"It's the least I can do. You saved my life. Just give me two minutes so I can get back to the others."

Before Dan could reply, the girl had *clicked* the door closed. He watched as she slipped away from them and disappeared around the warehouse. Once she'd gone, he inserted the key into the ignition and drew a breath.

Stay cool.

Dan turned the key. The engine sprang to life around them, and he locked the doors.

"Hold on, Quinn," he said.

He threw the vehicle into drive and hit the accelerator, launching the car across the dirt lot. Before he knew it, he was careening out from behind the building and into the heart of the property. He kept the lights off and aimed straight for the gate.

To his right, he saw several doors fly open from the main building, a stream of figures spill out from inside.

"Daddy! Are we going to make it?"

"I sure hope so! Hold on and buckle your seatbelt!"

He headed for the section in between the two entrance gates, praying that the force of the impact would split them apart, and then braced himself in his seat. The car collided with the metal and continued through it, separating the fence with a clatter. The station wagon plowed out into the night, roaring away from the lumberyard and the people running behind them.

When they'd cleared the vicinity, Dan turned to look behind him.

"Are you all right?"

"I'm fine, Dad."

"Did they hurt you?"

"No."

He exhaled, watching the rearview and the

road behind them. Although he was certain that Reginald would follow, he was confident that they'd gotten a good head start. In no time they'd reached an adjacent road, and Dan swerved down it, taking a shortcut to avoid the main thoroughfares.

Up above him, the sky glowed a magnificent blue, and the stars shined a fluorescent light from the heavens. One star in particular shone brighter than the others, and he took a second to admire it, once again thankful to be alive.

"Where are we going, Daddy?"

"I think it's time to find Aunt Meredith."

Although he couldn't see her face, he could hear Quinn breathing a sigh of relief in the backseat.

PART THREE
REBUILD

19

MEREDITH HAD NEVER LIKED DRIVING in the dark. The roads always seemed narrower than in the daytime, and the painted white and yellow lines reminded her of a maze. As she left the town of Settler's Creek behind, she did her best to focus on the road, but found her gaze wandering to the fields around her.

At any minute, she expected a legion of former townspeople to crop up in front of her, blocking the road and clambering for the vehicle.

So far the path had been clear.

She peered over at John, who was throwing cautious looks out the window. The nearest town was Coventry, and though they were halfway there, she had a sinking feeling that things wouldn't be much different.

In any case, she had another destination in mind: the Texas border.

Regardless of how the infection had travelled, there were bound to be military personnel there, and hopefully, medical assistance. She tried to dispel the rumors she'd heard about the border — about people being turned away, or worse — and convince herself that they'd find help.

She squinted at the road ahead, her vision

blurring. Meredith was exhausted. Ever since she woke up in the morning, the day had been a jumble of horrific events, and she still hadn't had a chance to digest them all.

She didn't know if she ever would.

The road took a slight curve, and a sign sprang into view. John jolted at the sight of it; Meredith's pulse quickened. They'd reached the Coventry limits. Although they were in no immediate danger, they were both on edge.

Before long they passed the first houses on the edge of town. From the looks of it, the lights were still on: Coventry had power. Meredith slowed the truck and glanced in the windows, watching spastic shadows roam back and forth from within.

Things weren't looking good.

"Keep going," John said, his voice somber.

She adjusted her foot from the brake to the gas, picking up speed again. The deeper into town they got, the more prevalent the houses and buildings became. Instead of providing relief, the sight of civilization brought more anxiety; multitudes of creatures wandered outside, hungry and on the prowl.

A few of them flung their bodies at the vehicle as Meredith drove by, and she did her best to avoid any knee-jerk reactions at the wheel. The last thing she needed was to lose control. If she crashed the pickup, the things would be on them in seconds.

Although she was able to avoid most of them,

several connected with the vehicle, and each time she jumped. She'd given John her rifle — his was out of bullets — and he held it next to the closed window.

By the time they'd reached the center of town, the streets had erupted in chaos. There were several abandoned vehicles in the road — the owners either gone or infected — and one of the buildings was aflame. Creatures spilled from the mouth of the burning structure, clawing at the yellow flames that surrounded them.

There were no survivors that Meredith could see.

She twisted the wheel, avoiding a pair of cars that had been left in the road.

"We need to get out of here," John said. "The last thing we need is to be trapped."

"Tell me about it."

She navigated between the wreckage, doing her best to avoid a collision, and turned down one of the lesser-known streets. Having grown up in the area, she knew the town almost as well as her own, and it was time to get out of it.

In a few minutes she'd cleared the town center and was heading westward. The border was just a few miles away.

Junked vehicles lined the roadway; creatures ambled in nearby fields.

"Do you think anyone will be there?" Meredith asked.

"The last I heard the roads were sealed off and

they weren't letting anyone through. That was almost a day ago, though. This whole thing came on so quick. Who knows what it will be like now."

"Everything just happened so fast...first Sheila, then Ben and Marcy, the doctor..."

Meredith's eyes welled up. John lowered the rifle and reached over to comfort her.

"There's nothing else you could have done, Meredith."

"I know," she whispered. "I just wish this whole thing was over and things would go back to normal."

"It can't go on like this forever," he said. "Something has to give."

Meredith could see the border approaching from a distance — a plethora of colored and flashing lights on the horizon. Rather than driving faster, she reduced her pace, suddenly aware that reaching it could mean danger or death as much as help or assistance.

There was no way to know.

To her relief, John seemed more alert than he had all night. He sat straight in his chair, Meredith's rifle propped on his leg. His eyes bore into the night like two dark coals, scanning the distance from the vehicle's interior.

No matter what the future brought, one thing

was clear: Meredith would need all the help she could get.

The flashing yellows, blues, and reds grew from dots to bulbs, and before she knew it she was upon them, the pickup crunching to a halt on the asphalt. She kept a distance of fifty feet, the headlights splashing onto the scene before them.

The border between Texas and Oklahoma on I-40 consisted of a three-lane highway on each side, with a dirt-encrusted median in the center. Above it was a perpendicular bridge that rose about fifty feet in the air. Normally traffic flowed through the area without impediment, crossing between states without issue or restriction.

Now the road before them was completely sealed off.

A row of military tanks, trucks, and police cars lined the street, creating a barricade that extended through the median. Cars had been abandoned on the roadside; doors and trunks left open, the owners nowhere in sight. Meredith stared into the lights, searching for signs of rescue. As she did, the lights seemed to grow brighter, more invasive.

In order to gain visibility, she'd have to move closer. She'd just started to roll forward when a voice rang into the night, sending her foot flying back to the brake.

"Drop your weapon and exit the vehicle!"

She jumped slightly and glanced over at John. He held the rifle steadfast, as if reluctant to give it up.

"Put it down, John," she whispered. "We don't want to get shot."

He sighed nervously and lowered the weapon.

The voice called out again—from the sounds of it, the person was speaking through a bullhorn, perhaps the speakers of a cruiser. John rolled down the window and tossed the rifle into the street. It hit with a clatter.

"Stay here, Meredith. I'll talk to them."

He gave her a reassuring stare, but she could see that his hands were shaking. Before she could protest, he opened the passenger's door and stepped out onto the pavement. She watched as he took a hesitant step toward the lights.

No sooner had he started moving than the voice returned.

"Stay where you are! Don't come any closer!"

The person did their best to sound firm and commanding, but Meredith could hear a timbre of fear. John froze in place, awaiting instructions.

Meredith peered through the glare, but could make out only blurred shapes. She heard the distant crackle of a radio, the purr of an engine. It was impossible to discern the voice's origin.

Something was off.

It should be obvious John wasn't infected. He'd followed the person's orders, after all, and he was standing in the street unarmed. Why wasn't anyone coming to greet him?

"We need help!" John shouted.

His words echoed into the street and died. For

a minute Meredith was convinced that they were alone, that the voice had been a figment of their imaginations. John took a step forward and raised his hands higher.

"We're just looking for a doctor! For some information! Please!"

The lights pulsed brighter. The radio fizzed from afar.

And then gunshots filled the air.

Meredith screamed, clutching the side of her head. Through the windshield, she saw John dive to the ground, saw bullets searing the ground around him. He screamed something at her, but his words were muffled, and she was unable to make them out.

This can't be happening. Not now. Not after all we've been through.

She reached for the door handle and flung open the door. She needed to get to John. She needed to help him.

Bullets pelted the other side of the metal, shaking it on its hinges. She cried out and ducked back into the car, bumping the steering wheel with her head. Pain coursed through her skull, and all of a sudden she was crying — shaking and crying — and the windshield was shattering above her.

Why were they doing this? Why would someone shoot without provocation?

Meredith tried to make sense of it all, but there was no sense to be had. Glass spilled against the console, and shards dug into her hair and hands.

"John!" she shrieked.

Was he still alive? Where was he?

Meredith reached for the shifter and put the vehicle into drive. She poked her head up, hoping to get a glimpse of him, and saw John on the ground. It looked like he was moving.

He's alive. I just need to get to him.

She hit the gas and rolled forward and positioned the car between the shooter and her fallen companion. The gunfire had ceased. Was the man reloading? Was he taking better aim? Knowing she didn't have much time, she lunged over into the passenger's seat and flung open the door, revealing John's startled face in front of her.

"Get in!" she screamed.

John pushed himself to his knees and scrambled inside, slamming the door shut behind him. Meredith hit the gas.

Behind them, the gunfire continued in short bursts, tearing into the trunk of the vehicle. She swerved from left to right, terrified that the shooter might hit a tire, and dipped her head below the steering wheel.

Her feet and hands felt like rubber; she fought to maintain control. When she'd gained about fifty feet of distance from the barricade, she sat up.

Tears streaked her face, and she struggled to breathe.

In the rearview, she watched the lights disappearing behind them, winking off one by one as if to remind them of all the people they'd lost.

T.W. Piperbrook

20

THE MOUNTAIN ROADS WERE CURVED and worn, but a welcome reprieve from the tattered streets of St. Matthews. Given the obstacles that Dan and Quinn had encountered the past few days, the dangers of nature seemed pale in comparison, and he took the turns with the ease of someone who'd driven them many times before.

Because of his familiarity with the area, Dan had taken the shortest possible route to the town's edge, and thus far, he'd seen no signs of being pursued. With each passing mile he was more confident that they'd lost Reginald and his group. Despite Reginald's vendetta against him, he was pretty sure the man had given up.

The risk of attack or infection surely outweighed the need to chase them down.

While driving, he'd had Quinn turn on the overhead lights and check the backseat for their belongings. While their personal items had been left untouched, the food had been taken. His daughter had only located one box in the backseat—an errant package that had somehow escaped discovery.

Other than that, they were without food or drink.

In addition, all of their weapons had been cleared out except for a lone pistol Dan had stashed underneath the seat.

All these things were bad, but they could've been worse. Dan and Quinn could have been tortured, killed, or infected. And yet they were alive. Having escaped imprisonment, Dan did his best to focus on the mission at hand.

Get to Meredith Tilly's, no matter what the cost.

After Quinn had finished checking the vehicle, he had her climb up into the front seat and buckle herself in. While searching in the backseat, she'd located her teddy bear, and she squeezed the animal with both arms, as if afraid to let it go again.

The two rode in relative quiet, breaking the silence only a few times to inquire on each other's comfort. Within a few hours of traveling, Dan glanced over to find his daughter asleep.

Before long the sun had poked through the trees, providing whispers of safety and freedom. Dan picked up the pace as the roads leveled out, carrying them one step closer to their destination.

I-40 sprawled out in the distance, intersecting with the mountain road, and he felt a shiver creep through his veins. He could already see the detritus and debris that lined both sides of the highway, and he had a sinking feeling that their journey would soon be stalled.

At the base of the road was a single stop sign. He

pulled to a stop to gauge the safest route of travel. The interstate reminded him of the town they'd come from, only compressed and contained — cars piled against one another, RV's overturned, and belongings smashed and scattered, all trapped within a space too small to hold them.

Unless he was to drive over the wreckage, Dan could see no way around it. The only other option was to drive off the road and into the desert; by the looks of it, several had tried and failed.

He glanced down at the shifter, which sported the option of four-wheel-drive. Then he studied his daughter's sleeping form next to him. If the station wagon were to get stuck, they'd be stranded on the open road with no access to shelter. On the other hand, they'd already come this far, and he doubted things would get any easier. Regardless of the risks, he had an obligation to get his daughter to safety.

He engaged the lever and rolled forward into the desert, trading the hum of the pavement for the crunch of compacted sand.

The tires of the Subaru Outback groaned in protest as they propelled the vehicle over the bristled underbrush. Although Dan did his best to create a clear path, avoiding nature was impossible. Every few feet, small shrubs and bushes scraped the exterior, and rocks pummeled the undercarriage.

If he'd been driving a truck or an SUV, navigation would have been easier, but he'd make do with what he had.

After a few minutes, the rumble awakened his daughter, and Quinn stared at him with wide eyes, frightened by the noise.

"It's OK," he said, reassuring her.

He returned his hands to the wheel, steering clear of a fallen motorcycle. The rider still clung to the handlebars, his legs missing below the knees.

Dan kept as close to the highway as he could. To lose sight of it would be to lose track of their whereabouts. Even with their bearings intact, the journey would be difficult enough.

After several miles of rocky terrain the desert leveled and smoothed, and Dan was able to focus on the interstate, looking for a way back on. Quinn had been keeping watch as well. She pointed to an open area beside two overturned sedans.

"Daddy, maybe we can get back on there!"

Dan concurred. A few seconds later, he drove the car over the lip of the asphalt and back onto the interstate. Although there were still some obstacles, the driving was manageable, and Dan appreciated the return to pavement.

Having traversed the White Mountains, the remainder of their journey was flat and straight. From memory, Dan recalled that I-40 ran adjacent to Settler's Creek; they would just need to travel the two hundred miles to get there.

The sun was still inching up the horizon,

revealing more and more of its form, and bands of light penetrated the vehicle's interior. Dan squinted from the glare, doing his best to make out the road ahead. By his guess it was about six in the morning.

He'd just lowered the sun visor when he saw something ahead; something moving several hundred feet away. Quinn had noticed it too, and she shot up straight in her seat, pointing at the source.

"What's that?" she asked.

From what Dan could tell, it was a passenger van; two figures were moving on the rooftop. As the station wagon crept closer, the occupants had hunkered down, doing their best to remain unnoticed.

"It looks like people," he said.

"Are you sure?"

He gave her a sideways glance, noting the fear in her eyes. On their current course they'd be passing within several feet of the stopped vehicle. Although it didn't appear the figures on top were infected, he couldn't be certain, and he didn't want to take any chances.

He shot a look off the highway, contemplating taking to the desert once again. It wasn't his preferred method of travel, but it would be better to be safe than sorry. He moved the vehicle into the slow lane, approaching the edge of the highway, and prepared to leave the road.

No sooner did he make the maneuver than he

saw something gleaming from the rooftop of the van. It looked like the two figures were holding something.

Was it a gun?

"Get down, Quinn!" he yelled.

He wrenched the car to the right, peeling off the road and into the dirt beside the highway. The car kicked up a barrage of silt and stone, and Dan cursed himself for the noise. The people remained in place. No gunshots sounded.

He continued to drive the vehicle forward, running in tandem with the highway, but keeping a fifty-foot buffer zone from the road and the people on it. When they passed the van, the two figures took to their feet and waved their hands. He saw that it was an older man and a woman, and their clothes were dirty and disheveled.

Dan slowed the vehicle to a halt in the desert.

Quinn was still holding her head between her knees. When the car stopped, she leaned up to peek over the dashboard.

The engine idled. A plume of dust surrounded the car on all sides, wafting into the air and obscuring their view of the interstate. Dan retrieved the pistol and cracked the window.

About fifty feet away, the two people were making their dismount from the van. The man was watching them from the rooftop while the woman climbed down a metal ladder at the back. Dan eyed them with caution. Although they seemed well intentioned, he knew better than to trust anyone.

He'd already learned that the hard way.

The two people departed the van and walked toward the station wagon. Instead of getting out of the vehicle to greet them, Dan remained in his seat, gun cocked out the window, ready to transfer his foot from brake to gas at the slightest hint of trouble.

As the dust cleared, he got a better look at them. Both were in their mid-fifties and had gray hair and weathered, lined faces. The man was wearing a button-up shirt and long pants; the woman was dressed in jeans and a t-shirt. Even from ten feet away, it was impossible to demarcate the colors — both travelers were covered in a residue of dust and dirt that seemed to penetrate both clothes and skin. In fact, the more he glared at them, the harder it was to tell where garments ended and flesh began. The man had a pair of binoculars around his neck.

When the two had come within ten feet of the vehicle, they stopped abruptly, noticing the gun pointed at them through the window.

"Please..." the man said, holding his hands in the air. "We don't want any trouble."

"Are you armed?" Dan asked.

The two of them shook their heads in unison. He looked them up and down but saw no sign that they were lying. He instructed them to back away from the vehicle, then stepped out to join them, keeping his pistol ready.

"Where are you headed?" he asked them.

The man and woman exchanged a worried glance, then pointed west, the way Dan and Quinn had come from.

"We're trying to reach our son," the woman said, blinking back tears.

The man reached over and took the woman's hand, squeezing it tight.

"We've been on the road for days. Our son lives in Phoenix, and we've been doing our best to reach him."

"We're from Oklahoma," the man explained. "At first we stayed put and watched the news, but after a while we couldn't take it anymore. We haven't heard from Isaac in over a week, and we needed to do something."

Dan nodded, feeling a wave of sympathy. He glanced back at his daughter, once again grateful that they were together.

"Where are you from?" the man asked.

"St. Matthews," Dan said, pointing behind him. "A little town over the mountains."

"How are things there?"

"Not good."

The man looked at his wife again, then cleared his throat. He reached into his pocket and pulled out a photo of a young man in his twenties with short dark hair.

"I know this is a long shot, but have you seen my son?"

The couple paused, both of them biting their lips in anticipation. Dan's eyes wandered to the interstate behind them, where a pair of bodies lined the road.

"I'm sorry, I haven't," he said.

The man and woman exhaled and pulled each other close. In this world of carnage, sometimes the best news was no news at all. The man let go of his wife's hand and pointed back at the van.

"Are either of you hungry?"

Dan furrowed his brow. In the last few hours, he and his daughter had already consumed the last bit of food that had been left in the station wagon. Even though he didn't feel like eating, his stomach felt hollow and empty, and he imagined his daughter probably felt the same way.

"Yes, but—"

"The food we have is safe," the man said. "It's wrapped up in red packages. You don't have to worry."

"We stole it from the men in white coats," the woman explained.

For the first time all day, Dan felt a surge of hope. He motioned for his daughter to join him, and when she exited the vehicle, the two of them followed the couple back to the van.

21

"M Y NAME'S ROBERTA SMITH," THE woman said. "And this is my husband Ken."

The woman sat cross-legged in the back of the van, and she smiled at Dan and Quinn with warmth they hadn't seen in a while. The man was digging through a backpack he had stashed there, and he pulled out several packages of dried fruits and passed them out to the group.

"When I saw you two driving up the road, I hid all our things," the man explained.

He stuck out a grimy hand, and Dan took it. Dan introduced him and his daughter.

"I'm Dan, and this is my daughter Quinn."

"Quinn! What a pretty name!" Roberta said.

The little girl blushed as she dug into her apple slices. Dan surveyed the back of the van. At one time it'd contained several rows of seats, but it appeared they'd been removed. A sleeping bag lined the floor, and several items of clothes had been scattered across the interior.

"Is this your vehicle?" Dan asked.

"No, we found it here. We've mostly been traveling on foot. We lost our vehicle back in Texas when we got a flat tire. Within minutes we were swarmed by the infected, and we barely made it out alive. Since then we've been camping out during the day and making our progress at night."

"It's been dangerous with those men in white coats out there," Roberta added. "We came across one of their vans when they weren't around. That's how we got this food."

Ken held up the backpack he'd been rifling through.

"It didn't take us long to figure out what was going on. We're pretty sure the infection is spread through the food and water supply."

Dan nodded, surprised at their astuteness. While he ate his food, he ran through the events in St. Matthews: the start of the infection, their run-ins with the agents, and their escape from town. He did his best to narrate the story without rehashing the violence, and he left out the part about Julie. Quinn had been through enough. The last thing he wanted to do was reopen the wound.

While he was talking, the Smiths shook their heads in disbelief. From the sounds of it, they'd left Oklahoma before things got bad; most of the troubles they'd encountered had been on the road.

"I just hope we find Isaac soon." Roberta lowered her eyes.

"We'll find him, honey," Ken said. "No matter how long it takes."

The couple held hands again. In spite of what was happening, it was obvious they'd drawn strength from each other, and Dan couldn't help but think of his own wife. What would it have been like if they'd survived together? He could only imagine that Julie would be as strong as Roberta. He felt a pang of sorrow, and he did his best to swallow it with the last of his fruit.

Ken finished his meal and wandered to the front of the vehicle. Dan watched as the man pressed the binoculars to his eyes, rotating the lenses back and forth over the ruined road.

"I haven't seen any of the infected in a while," Ken said. "It's probably been a day since we ran into one of them."

"I wonder if they're dying out," Dan suggested. "Maybe the infection is running its course."

"We can only hope."

The two exchanged a wry smile.

"So where are you headed?" Ken asked.

"We're headed to Oklahoma to find my sister-in-law. She lives in Settler's Creek, just over the Texas border. We're hoping nothing's hit there yet."

"Well, everything seemed OK when we left. But we've run into a few people on the road since, and it sounds like it's spreading."

Dan swallowed the lump in his throat. Ever since leaving the salvage yard, he'd clung steadfast to the goal of reaching Meredith, hoping to find safe haven. If the virus had truly spread into Oklahoma—and more specifically, Settler's Creek—then their travels would be for naught.

Sensing his anxiety, Ken put a hand on his shoulder.

"Everything will work out, Dan. Have faith."

The older man had put down his binoculars and smiled. Despite his tattered clothes and dirt-stained face, his eyes radiated a sense of hope. Dan did his best to smile back.

"We should probably get going soon. We've troubled you folks enough."

"Nonsense. You're not leaving until we give you some food for the road."

Dan wrinkled his brow. "There's no way I could take anything from you."

"I insist. You have a daughter to feed, Dan, and the last thing I'd want is for the two of you to starve."

Ken walked past Dan and to the back of the van. He picked up his backpack and tossed it to his wife. She picked it up without hesitation.

"Roberta, would you mind packing up some food for these folks? I'm going to keep my eyes peeled out front."

"Sure thing."

Ken gave her a loving smile before returning to his post.

The older woman sifted through the contents of the bag, pulling out several tightly wrapped packages and placing them on the floor. On the floor behind her was another backpack. She dumped out the contents and began to fill it with the things she'd sorted for Dan and Quinn.

"You don't have to do this."

"It's the least we can do. You've given us a lot of insight on what's in store for us on the road ahead, and for that we are grateful. Anything that helps us to find Isaac is a huge help."

When the woman was finished, she handed the packed bag to Quinn. The little girl hefted it in her hands and gave her a smile.

"Are we leaving, Daddy?"

"Yes, we should really get going."

Dan patted his pocket, ensuring he had his keys, and then looked toward one of the side windows. He peeked around one of the drawn shades, spotting the station wagon in the distance. Everything looked as it did before.

No sooner had he let down the shade than Ken's voice rang from the driver's seat.

"I wouldn't leave just yet."

"What do you mean?"

"There's trouble headed our way."

Even before he took sight of it, Dan could hear the rumble of a vehicle in the desert. The noise was loud and undeniable, and it made his heart hammer in his chest. For the past half an hour, he'd been given a subtle reprieve from the dangers of the road, but now his survival instincts were knocking louder than ever.

"Stay down!" he hissed to Quinn and Roberta.

The two huddled behind the passenger's seat, their eyes roaming the vehicle. Ken had stooped below the dashboard. Dan crawled up to meet him.

"Who is it?" he whispered.

Ken looked over at him. The shine in his eyes had long since faded; in its place was an expression of worry.

"I'm not sure. I don't think it's the agents, and it certainly isn't the creatures. Whoever it is doesn't look friendly."

Dan had already withdrawn his weapon. He snuck a glance over the dashboard, keeping his head as low as possible.

The vehicle was approaching from the west. By the shape and size, he was unable to get a read on the make and model.

"Can I borrow the binoculars?"

Ken handed them to him and he held the lenses to his face. With the vehicle magnified, he was able to make out more of the structure. It appeared to be an SUV—similar to the ones used by the agents—but the sides had been reinforced with metal brackets, and knives and pieces of sharp metal had been attached to the exterior. The hood had been spray-painted with graffiti.

Hanging out the windows were several men in dirt-stained fatigues. They whooped into the air as the vehicle advanced, their eyes roving the littered highway.

At present they were about a half-mile away,

but soon they'd be upon the station wagon that Dan had left parked in the desert. He grimaced and shook his head. Although he wasn't certain who they were, it was clear that they were up to no good.

He'd seen their type before, but usually on the other end of a pair of handcuffs.

He looked over at the man next to him.

"Ken, I need you to go in back with the girls."

The man took his instruction without argument, clambering into the back of the van. Dan inched backward, positioning himself behind the passenger's seat, and kept his gun at chest level. If they were lucky, the men in fatigues would pass by without detecting them.

At the same time, he knew better than to expect it.

The roar of the engine grew louder, as did the cries. In another situation, the men might have been a group of friends on a road trip, a circle of comrades out for a night on the town.

Not now.

Dan watched them with growing dread. If they were to be discovered, they'd be outmatched. By the looks of it, there were four men in the vehicle, and not one of them appeared friendly.

He cast a quick look behind him. The others were huddled on the floor. The mini-van contained several windows, but all of them had curtains and shades, and all of them were covered. He noticed the sleeping bag and clothes on the floor, and he motioned toward them.

"Hide underneath," he hissed to his companions.

The three people behind him scurried underneath the belongings. Even with the garments over them, they were hardly concealed — anyone who happened upon them would surely inspect the van further.

He turned his attention back out the front window. The SUV had stopped beside a pickup truck. The two men in back jumped out, jeering into the air. He saw that they carried assault rifles in their hands. Both had unkempt beards and baseball caps; one of them was wearing a stained white jacket rather than fatigues.

Although they didn't appear to be agents, they carried both the armament and the clothing of those responsible for the infection. Apparently these men had overpowered some of the agents; by the looks of it, they'd taken their vehicle and their gear.

The two men approached the pickup and tore open the doors. A dead body spilled out from inside and onto the highway, collapsing in a pile of limbs. The man in the white jacket — the pseudo agent — fired at the corpse with his rifle, his laughter spilling into the air. The other man hopped into the driver's seat and threw a handful of loose objects out the side, scattering coins, papers, and clothing across the pavement.

Apparently finding nothing of interest, the men moved on to the bed of the truck. They peered into the cab, dragging the tips of their rifles along the edge.

There were three vehicles in between the pickup and the minivan — a Jeep, a sedan, and a sports car. Before long, the men would reach the vehicle Dan and his companions were hiding in and they'd be exposed. He watched in silence, mind racing.

He had six bullets in the gun he was holding. In order to use it, he'd need to get a drop on the men outside. If he started a firefight from within the vehicle, Ken, Roberta, and Quinn were likely to get hit in the crossfire.

He couldn't allow that to happen.

Outside, the two men on foot had moved on to the Jeep. The one in fatigues busted out the window with the end of his rifle and stared inside. The sound of glass shattering sent a ripple of fear through Dan's body.

He had to take action. If he didn't, he might not get another chance.

He climbed into the passenger's seat, then he cracked the door and jumped out onto the interstate.

22

EREDITH AND JOHN HELD HANDS as they traveled I-40. They were going the wrong way—eastbound in a westbound lane—but that was the least of their worries. Given the events they'd just lived through, they were lucky to be alive.

"How're you feeling, John?"

He shrugged and looked down at his wounded leg.

"I think I ripped a stitch. I might need your help again."

She smiled and squeezed his hand. Her fingers shook in his.

"No problem."

"I think we can rule out finding any help at the border."

"I just can't believe it. None of it makes any sense. Why would they shoot at us? You did everything they asked."

"They're probably scared, Meredith, the same as us."

The two rode in silence for several minutes. The wind gusted in through the shattered windshield, making it difficult to talk, and the open air made Meredith feel vulnerable and exposed.

Since leaving the border, the sun had crept above the distant plains, ushering in a brand new day. Meredith surveyed the road ahead, doing her best to lose herself in the landscape.

Along the edge of the highway she noticed several broken-down vehicles, doors hanging ajar, passengers missing. She wondered where the occupants had gone and whether they'd been infected. The roadside contained an endless maze of cornfields, and she could imagine the creatures roaming between the stalks in search of victims.

The image made her shudder.

"What should we do, John?" she asked.

"I think we should find a good place to lock down for a while."

"That's easier said than done. With the town in the state that it is, I can't think of a single place that might be safe."

"How about your house?"

Meredith paused. "You know, that might not be a bad idea. At least it's in a secluded area. That way if someone approaches we'll be able to see them."

"You said there was no one there when you left, right?"

"No. Everything was normal until I got to Sheila's house."

"If something looks amiss, we can always leave. But I think we need time to regroup."

Meredith agreed.

Having formulated a plan, the two fell into

silence once again. The scent of the surrounding fields filtered into the vehicle — a combination of grass, hay, and dirt — and Meredith huffed in a breath, doing her best to focus on getting home.

A few miles later they approached the exit for Coventry, and she took the turn, glad to rejoin the flow of traffic. The off-ramp was deserted, but she could see lights in the distance; a subtle reminder of what was waiting for them. Hours earlier, both Coventry and Settler's Creek had been brimming with creatures; she could only assume that things had gotten worse.

"You wouldn't happen to know any shortcuts, would you?" John asked her.

Meredith furrowed her brow. When they'd crossed town before, they'd at least had the protection of the front windshield, as well as several rifles. Now they had nothing.

Getting through town would be even more dangerous.

"I know an alternate route, but it hasn't been used in years."

"What is it?"

"State Route 63. It used to be a shortcut connecting Coventry to Settler's Creek, but I don't even think it's functional anymore. Last time I checked it was blocked off."

"Well, I'd say it's worth a try. The less of those things we see, the better."

"Agreed."

A few minutes down the road, prior to the

town limits, Meredith swung the pickup onto a hidden road in between two patches of field grass. It'd been years since she'd taken the route, but her memory served her well; before long, the truck tires were bouncing over the rugged asphalt. She clenched the wheel with both hands, staring at the forsaken road in front of them.

Weeds sprang from every crack, and yellowed grass marked its borders. It was as if nature had sensed a weakness and was intent on swallowing the pavement whole.

"You weren't kidding about this road," John mused.

"I told you it was a little rough around the edges."

"Didn't you say it was blocked off?"

"I thought so."

As if in response, a gated barrier became visible in the distance. A minute later, Meredith tapped the brake and the pickup ground to a halt.

On either side of the road were cement blocks; between them was a large metal pole. On foot, the barrier would be no obstacle—they'd simply duck underneath. In a car they'd have to drive around.

"Time for a little off-roading," Meredith said.

She yanked the steering wheel to the left and pulled into the overgrowth, field grass whipping at the vehicle's exterior. Once they'd gained clearance, she started swerving toward the road.

She was so preoccupied that she didn't notice the upcoming car until John warned her.

"Look out!" he yelled.

She mashed the brake, stopping just inches shy of a Camaro parked in the middle of the field. Her body jolted back and forth against the seatbelt.

"What the hell?"

Both John and Meredith stared out the broken windshield at the phantom vehicle. Because of its low height and the length of the weeds, she'd failed to notice it.

Although the vehicle was white, the paint job had faded. The exterior was chipped and cracked, and there was a dent on the bumper. The rear window was dark and tinted, and although Meredith did her best to see through it, she was unable to make out anything inside. The trunk was slightly ajar, and it shifted up and down with the gust of a distant breeze.

John shifted uncomfortably.

"We should back up and go around it, get the hell out of here."

"I'm not sure I can do that, John."

"What do you mean? Why not?"

"I know who this car belongs to."

Meredith stared at the back of the Camaro for a solid minute before deciding to get out. Between the make, model, and the license plate, she'd instantly recognized the vehicle as belonging to one of the shop owners in Settler's Creek.

The owner's name was Mark Robins.

If Mark had somehow survived the infection, it would make sense that he would have driven outside of town for help. What didn't make sense was why he'd chosen to stop here.

She studied the vehicle warily, expecting the man to emerge, but the car remained silent. Undeterred, she reached for the door handle, intending to seek the man out. If he was in trouble, she needed to help.

"Meredith, please stay here," John said.

"I know the owner. This is Mark Robins' car. I need to make sure he's OK."

Ignoring the warning of her companion, she lifted the handle and jumped out into the grass. From the other side of the vehicle, she heard John follow suit. His feet crunched through the grass, and he met her at the Camaro's trunk.

She gave him a worried look.

"Mark? Are you in there?" she called.

She paused for a response, but heard only the wind whipping through the tall grass around her. From somewhere overhead, a bird emitted a single cry.

"Mark?"

She spun in a circle and scanned the fields around them, but saw no one approaching. She took a step toward the driver's side of the Camaro. Although it was possible the man had wandered off into the grass, she had the instinctive feeling that he was inside.

John tailed close behind. She took another step.

When she got to the driver's side window, her mouth hung open. Mark was hunched over the steering wheel, unmoving. It looked like he was dead. She cried out and reached for the door handle.

"Mark! Oh my God!"

John lunged to stop her, but before he had a chance, she'd whipped open the door. The man inside was lifeless, still.

And then, without warning, he wasn't.

The man turned his head to face them, his cheek still pressed against the steering wheel. His eyes were red and glossy, his cheeks filled with veins. He opened his mouth to speak, and to Meredith's surprise, a set of words escaped.

"Help me," he muttered.

His voice was cracked, barely audible. At the sound of his words, Meredith dropped to her knees and leaned into the Camaro.

"Mark? What happened to you?" she whispered.

Tears slid from her eyes. She'd known Mark for years. As the sole proprietor of the town's convenience store, she'd always known him to be boisterous and larger than life. Even in the hardest times, he was the first one to crack a joke, the first one to make the townsfolk smile. To see him in this condition—weak and in the throes of death—was more than she could handle.

The man attempted to respond, but his words

were dull and muted. Meredith scoured his body for injuries. Other than his appearance, he seemed untouched.

"Stay back, Meredith. He's infected."

Although she heard John's words, she was unable to heed them. She'd already seen too many of the townsfolk die — she couldn't give up on Mark like all the others. Clearly he needed help. If she could just get him to a doctor, a hospital...

"Meredith!"

John tugged on her shoulder, pulling her away from the seemingly infected man. She covered her face with her hands and sobbed. Since speaking last, Mark had closed his eyes, and his head had slid down the steering wheel, sinking into his chest.

"I know how hard this is, but you have to step back."

John reached out and took her in his embrace. She rocked silently with him for several seconds, finding comfort in his arms, and tried to pretend that she was anywhere but here. When she closed her eyes, the world was normal, and everyone she knew was safe.

Sheila, Ben and Marcy, Mark, Julie...

Her illusion shattered with a scream. When she opened her eyes, Mark had shifted in his seat and was staring at them again. This time he was awake and alert, and his eyes blazed with violence.

"Watch out!"

John threw Meredith behind him just as the

man leapt from the Camaro. In less than a minute, Mark had been overtaken by infection, and he tackled John to the ground in a tangle of arms and legs.

Meredith screamed, but with little effect.

The friendly shop owner she'd known before was gone. In his place was a creature bent on their demise.

23

D AN'S PULSE CLIMBED AS HIS feet hit the pavement. The men in fatigues were only two car-lengths away. The SUV had stopped in the desert, and the driver watched his comrades intently, blowing a whiff of smoke in the air from a cigarette in his hand. The man in the passenger's seat stared in the other direction.

Dan was completely in the open, but he hadn't been seen.

Once the men noticed him they'd open fire. Of that he was certain. In order to protect his daughter and their two companions, he needed to lead the attackers away from the minivan.

Adjacent to the vehicle was another car, and he scurried across the pavement toward it. While he was running, he heard the two men on foot smash the remaining windows of the Jeep. His heart buckled.

Focus, Dan, focus.

If he were to have any chance at overtaking the men, he'd have to keep his calm and rely on his police training. Several lives depended on it. He made it to the back of the car, crouched next to the trunk, and held his gun ready.

After waiting several seconds, he poked his

head over the vehicle. The two men on foot had opened the doors of the Jeep and were rifling through the interior.

He needed to get farther away.

Behind him were several other vehicles. He scampered to the next one right as one of the men began to yell.

"Over there! I saw someone!"

"Now we're talking!" one of the men screamed. "And I was just getting bored."

Dan heard the patter of approaching feet, and he ducked behind the trunk, hunkering down as low as his body would allow.

"There he is!"

"I see him!"

A volley of bullets sprayed into the car behind him—a red station wagon—and Dan covered his head as the windshield shattered. When the noise stopped, he stood and fired a round at the two oncoming men. The bullet ricocheted off a nearby vehicle.

"He's armed!" one of the men screamed.

The two men ducked out of sight, using the cover of a blue hatchback. The SUV was at a dead stop, and the men inside were poking their guns out the window.

"There's only one of them!" the driver called.

That's right, Dan thought. *Come on.*

He crept on all fours to the back of the red station wagon, then darted to the next vehicle, making his way farther from the mini-van. Shouts and footfalls echoed from behind him; the men were in hot pursuit.

If he were lucky, maybe they'd run out of ammunition. Then he'd have a better chance at taking them down. As if in response, a burst of gunfire followed in his wake. He kept low to the ground, his breath heaving.

He had five shots of his own. Not nearly enough. He'd have to shoot for accuracy, and given that his targets were moving, that could prove difficult.

At the same time, Dan had been the best shot on the force. Back when Sheriff Turner had been alive, he'd often commended Dan on his accuracy at the shooting range, and the other officers had admired his skill.

He thought of his fallen comrades and felt his body flood with anger.

Clearly the men pursuing him had survived the infection, but rather than being grateful, they'd chosen to do others harm. The thought made him sick, and he clenched his teeth.

Dan leapt up from hiding and drew a bead on one of the approaching men. The man cried out in surprise, as if he'd been expecting his target to flee. Dan squeezed off a round, striking the man square in the chest. The man reeled to the pavement.

The second man was right behind the first. Before the man could react, Dan fired again, striking him in the forehead. The man tumbled backward, dropping his rifle to the ground with a clatter.

The men in the SUV had rolled from the desert to the road, navigating between several vehicles in an attempt to get to him. Rather than running, Dan ducked behind the blue hatchback and aimed at the oncoming vehicle.

The SUV stopped twenty feet away, and the man in the passenger's seat hung out the window.

"Looks like we have a little standoff here," the man chided.

The driver revved the engine. Dan pointed the pistol at the man.

"What do you want?" he asked.

The man snorted. "Nothing in particular. Just having a little fun." He made a noise in his throat and spit a wad of phlegm into the street. "Are you going to put that down and surrender, or are we gonna have to come after you?"

"Why are you doing this?"

The man shrugged. "Why not? You just killed two of *us*. And I bet it felt good, didn't it?"

"I shot them in self defense."

"Sure you did."

The driver revved the engine again. Dan glanced around him, taking in his options. There were several more cars behind him. He could make his way backward, putting some distance between him and the men. But then what? It was obvious they weren't going to leave until he was dead, and even then they still might search the surrounding vehicles.

The minivan remained still in the distance. He flicked his gaze toward it, wondering if his daughter was watching him right now, whether or not she was scared.

"Did you see that, Carl?" the man in the passenger's seat asked his friend. "He was looking at the minivan. I think you're right. I bet there are more of them in there. What do you say we leave this fucker and go check?"

The man stared at Dan, waiting for his reaction. Dan did his best to remain calm, though his heart was pounding. He eyed the men with his hand on the trigger. Even if he was outmatched and outgunned, he would do his best to stop them.

He couldn't let them get to his companions.

"How about this," the driver said. "If you give yourself up, we'll let the others go."

The man in the passenger's seat sneered at Dan; it was obvious he was lying.

"I don't think so," Dan responded.

He took careful aim, and before the man could retort, he fired off a shot and pierced the man in the neck. Blood seeped from the wound; his head sunk into his chest. The rifle fell from his grasp and hit the pavement.

Dan adjusted his aim to the driver, but the SUV had started moving in reverse, careening back out into the desert. He squeezed off several more rounds—his last—but they bounced uselessly off the hood of the vehicle.

Out of bullets, he watched helplessly as the SUV cruised westbound. It took him a second to realize what was happening. When he did, he sprinted frantically after it, lungs heaving.

The driver was on a collision course with the minivan.

Dan cast his pistol aside and raced after the moving vehicle. He screamed a warning to his companions, but his voice seemed thin, inadequate.

He envisioned Ken, Roberta, and Quinn hiding beneath the sleeping bag and blankets, oblivious to what was coming, and his stomach dropped.

The SUV barged forth, picking up speed. The tires kicked up dust around it; the engine soared. Although he couldn't see the driver, he imagined the man sneering as he aimed at the vehicle, ready to risk his own life to get to the other survivors.

Dan had never felt more powerless.

He watched in horror as the SUV collided with the side of the minivan, crunching into the exterior. The vehicle rocked on its axles from the impact; the side windows shattered. From somewhere inside, he heard the occupants scream.

He was only twenty feet away now, and he pushed his body as fast as he was able, suppressing the fear that he was too late.

The SUV tires continued to spin. Dan wondered if the man inside was still trying to do damage or if his foot was stuck on the gas.

He reached the driver's side door in a rage and ripped it open. The man inside was bruised and bloodied, and he was reaching for an assault rifle on the seat.

Dan grabbed him and threw him into the dirt. The man groaned in pain. It looked like he'd injured his leg. Dan retrieved the assault rifle and slammed the door shut. He pointed it at the man.

"One move and you're dead."

With the immediate threat alleviated, he raced to check on the occupants of the minivan.

He needed to find his daughter.

He raced to the driver's door and yanked, but the frame must've bent from the impact, and it wouldn't budge. He cupped his hand over his eyes and peered inside. There was no sign of the occupants.

"Quinn!" he shouted.

He tore around the front of the vehicle, afraid of what he might find on the other side. When he reached it, he panicked. Ken and Roberta were stooped down on the pavement. Quinn was in between them.

"Is she OK?"

Roberta looked up as he approached, her eyes filled with concern.

"She's fine. Just shaken up is all."

Dan knelt in front of her. Quinn looked up at

him, eyes brimming with tears, and then flung her arms around his neck. He held her close.

"I thought they shot you, Dad."

"I'm fine, honey, don't worry about me," he whispered. "Are you all right?"

"I'm OK."

"Were you inside when—?"

Roberta stood and interjected.

"Ken was watching what was going on. He already had the door open, and we were able to get out in time."

Dan glanced back at the minivan, where the side door was ajar. Through the opening he could see inside the interior; the driver's side had been crunched inwards like a bent can.

"Where's the driver?" Ken asked.

"I left him on the other side."

"I'll run and check on him."

The older man grabbed the assault rifle from Dan and got to his feet, then disappeared around the other side of the minivan. Dan remained on the ground with his daughter.

Each time they'd been separated, he'd felt a wave of guilt wash over him that was difficult to ignore. He hated leaving Quinn alone. Anytime she was in danger, he felt like a failure, like he'd made the wrong decision.

In spite of that, she'd managed to stay safe. In just a week she'd already grown up so much.

"You're a brave girl," he said to her. She looked

up at him with wet eyes, and he kissed her head. "I'm proud of you."

"I'm proud of you, too, Dad."

He gave her a squeeze and rose to his feet. Roberta was already standing, and she gave them a contagious smile.

"You two are lucky to have one another. I can tell you have a special bond, and it makes me happy to see it."

"Thanks, Roberta. I appreciate you taking care of her."

Dan surveyed the highway in both directions, half-expecting to see another truck or vehicle closing in, but the area remained quiet. A few seconds later he heard the trickle of conversation from the other side of the vehicle, and he assumed it was Ken and the SUV driver.

"I'll be back," he said to Quinn and Roberta.

He stalked around the vehicle to the other side. The driver of the SUV was still on the ground. Ken had the weapon trained on him.

"I think his leg's broken," Ken said.

The man groaned in response, as if to confirm the theory. His leg was bent unnaturally and he clutched it with both hands.

"Help me," the man whispered.

Dan stared at the man, feeling his chest tighten with rage. He pictured his daughter in the minivan, what would have happened if Ken hadn't seen the SUV coming. Although the impact may not have killed her, she would've been seriously injured.

"After what you've done, we have every right to leave you here."

"You can't. I-I need a doctor."

Dan glared at the man. "You're on your own."

"You can't leave me here."

"Watch me."

"I'll take him."

Dan looked up in surprise. Ken had lowered the weapon, and he breathed a sigh.

"Me and Roberta will do our best to get him help."

"I don't think that's a good idea, Ken. With his broken leg, he'll be unable to walk. If you come across those things, they'll be on you in seconds."

"We can always drive."

Ken's eyes switched from Dan's face to the SUV; Dan followed his stare. Despite the collision, the front end appeared to be intact. By the looks of it, the bumper had absorbed most of the damage.

"Let me see if it's still drivable."

Dan walked over to the vehicle and jumped inside. The keys were still in the ignition. He fired the engine and put the car in reverse. The minivan groaned as the bumper dislodged from its side, but Dan was able to pull the car away.

"I'm no mechanic, but it seems OK," he called out to Ken.

"Let me have a look," Ken said.

He popped the hood, and he and Ken checked the vehicle. Although it was impossible to be certain, it appeared that there was no mechanical damage, and no obvious leaks from the undercarriage. It appeared the vehicle was in working order. Dan smirked at the exterior – the body covered in metal plating, the knives fastened on the side, the graffiti on the hood.

"It's a beast, but it should get you where you need to go," Dan said. "In fact, the way they've rigged this thing, it's probably safer than my station wagon. It's higher off the ground, and with the weapons on the side..."

"Why don't you take it, Dan?"

"We already have the – "

"We'll take the station wagon. You need to protect your daughter."

"But you'll have the extra passenger..."

"It will be easier to get him in and out. I mean it. Take the SUV."

Dan looked back out into the desert, where his Subaru Outback sat in the dirt and sand. In spite of its sentimental value, he was being offered something safer, and right now, he needed all the security he could get.

"Thank you, Ken."

"No need to thank me. You've helped us more than we've helped you. You've saved our lives. And we're forever grateful."

The girls had emerged from the other side of the vehicle. Quinn ran to Dan's side, embracing him, and Roberta joined her husband. Dan smiled at the couple.

"I wish you nothing but the best of luck in finding Isaac."

"Thanks, Dan, we really appreciate it. I know we'll find him. We have faith."

The group exchanged hugs, and then they all began to pack the vehicles.

24

MEREDITH WATCHED HELPLESSLY AS THE creature—the shop owner she'd once known as Mark Robins—overpowered John and pinned him on the grass. For the moment John was holding it at bay, but Meredith knew it was only a matter of time until the thing broke loose and tore into him.

All around her were empty fields; no sign of any weapons.

The Camaro. Mark has to have something in there.

She ducked into the parked car and searched frantically, but found nothing except clothes and food wrappers. The vehicle smelled of sweat and cigarette butts, and she recoiled at the odor. Outside the vehicle, John grunted as he fended the creature off, the creature hissing on top of him.

She leapt back out of the Camaro, suddenly remembering the open trunk.

There could be a weapon inside.

She ran the three steps to the rear of the vehicle and threw it open. What she saw made her gasp. Lying in the trunk, a knife lodged in her forehead, was the body of Sarah Robins, Mark's wife. Her face was pale and contorted, her eyes possessed. Next to her was a shovel.

Mark must have come to bury her.

Meredith choked on her bile and grabbed the shovel, fearing that the dead woman would lash out and take hold of her, but the woman remained still. Weapon in hand, she rushed back to John's aid.

One of the creature's hands had broken free from John's grasp, and it flailed wildly at his face. She raised the shovel and brought it down on the thing's back. The metal struck its skin with a deep *thud*, but the creature continued to attack.

She backed up and swung again. This time she connected with its head, knocking the thing sideways and onto the grass. John scrambled to his feet and out of reach.

Meredith advanced on the creature, the shovel held high above her head. The creature — the man she'd once known as Mark Robins — glared at her with empty eyes from the ground.

She started to swing, then stopped. All she could see was the man she'd known for years, the man who'd joked and bantered with his customers as he rang up their purchases. Mark was one of the most harmless people she'd known. What must it have been like for him to have to kill his infected wife? Had he known he was infected himself?

John came up beside her and reached for the shovel. The creature hissed at them from the ground.

"Do you need me to — ?"

She stared at Mark, who'd already risen to a crouch, arms poised to strike.

"No, I've got it," Meredith said.

She arched the shovel back over her head and swung as hard as she could. This time she didn't stop until the creature was dead.

"Are you OK?" John asked.

"I'm fine."

Meredith stared at the road ahead, her eyes wide and unblinking. On the horizon was an endless sea of grass. The asphalt was even more cracked and covered than before, and the pickup jolted and bounced as she drove.

"I can only imagine what you're going through," John said. "You've known these people a lot longer than I have."

"My whole life."

Meredith swallowed, her gaze drifting over the distant fields.

"I'm sorry all of this happened."

"Do you have any idea what this feels like, John? To have to do this to people you knew? People you loved?" she asked.

"I can't say that I do."

"Of course you don't."

John paused.

"I'm here for you, Meredith," he said.

Meredith glanced over at him, her hands

trembling. For some reason, instead of the man she'd once loved, all she saw was the man who had betrayed her.

"Like you were before? When you lied to me?"

John went silent.

"You hurt me, John."

"I know, and I feel awful about it. If I could take it all back — do things differently — I would. I should've told you the truth."

"Damn right you should've."

Even though it wasn't the time or place, Meredith couldn't suppress the swell of anger. She tried to tell herself that it was the adrenaline rush of what had happened to Mark — or perhaps the shock from what had happened to Sheila, Ben, Marcy, and the doctor. Whatever the case, she was unable to stop the words from tumbling from her mouth.

"Why couldn't you have told me the truth sooner?"

"I was afraid of what you might think. That you might...look at me differently. All I wanted was a fresh start. To leave the past behind."

"Have you seen her since?"

"No. That was the only time. We signed the papers, Meredith. It's over with."

Meredith felt her breathing slow to normal. Out of the corner of her eye, she saw John reaching for her hand and she let him take it. He squeezed her fingertips; his hand was firm and warm.

"I'm sorry, Meredith — for all of this, for

everything. I know this isn't the time or place to discuss this, but I want a chance to start over, for real this time."

She looked over at him. He was staring at her intently, his brown eyes containing the same warmth as when she met him. Before she knew it her anger had dimmed, and in its place was a wave of guilt.

"Me too," she said finally. "Maybe I overreacted. It's just that...I've been hurt before, and I couldn't stand to be hurt again."

"You didn't overreact at all. I deserved it."

"I should've let you explain. But I was so... *angry* that you'd lied to me, that I couldn't see past it." She sighed. "All of that seems so irrelevant now."

He nodded.

"From now on, John, no more lies."

"You saved my life, Meredith. If telling the truth is what you want, that's the least I can do."

John gave her a smile, then leaned over and kissed her cheek.

"I love you, Meredith."

"I love you, too."

Several miles later the town appeared. Buildings reared their heads over adjacent fields, the sun glancing off their rooftops. Overhead, the birds sang and circled. From this distance, Settler's

Creek seemed calm and familiar, bearing little resemblance to the nightmarish warzone they'd encountered earlier.

But Meredith knew better.

Every so often she'd notice hints of movement between the buildings, a subtle reminder of the danger that lurked within. She counted her blessings that they'd been able to take an alternate route.

At this point, going into town would be a suicide mission.

Every so often, Meredith drove past an offshoot road that led into town, but she passed without stopping. Presumably they'd be blocked off too, which was just as well.

Since leaving behind Mark and the Camaro, they'd yet to see another car on the road.

When they reached the third such turn, Meredith continued driving, intent on passing by it. It wasn't until John spoke up that she hit the brake.

"Turn here," he said.

"How come? If we go a bit further, it will take us closer to my house and we can avoid more of the main roads."

"Trust me."

She turned the wheel just in time, changing course onto the side road, and smiled. For most of her life, Meredith had been the one making the decisions. But the events of the last day had left her physically and emotionally drained. It felt good to have someone to share the burden.

Much like the previous road, the street was weathered and worn. As they progressed down it, Meredith wrinkled her brow.

"Doesn't this come out near the furniture shop?"

John nodded.

"What if the infected are still there?"

"Hopefully they've left. We'll have to be careful."

"What are we going to do there?"

"Trust me."

Meredith fell silent. In spite of their rocky past, she *did* trust John; if he was taking her back to the furniture shop, there must be a reason.

A few minutes later they approached another barrier similar to the one they'd crossed before, and she swerved around it and into the grass. This time there were no cars buried on the other side, and soon they were back on the main road.

Meredith's arms prickled. The last time she'd been on this road, she was rushing to John's aid. For the past few miles she'd been able to dispel the thoughts of the infected, but now the memories came flooding back.

She swallowed and continued down the road.

Before she knew it, the furniture shop had appeared in the distance. She squinted against the sun's glare, but saw no shapes or shadows around the exterior.

"Maybe they're gone," she said out loud, as if saying the words would make them true.

"Hopefully."

John dug into the backseat and retrieved the shovel they'd taken from Mark's Camaro. In the absence of a gun, the garden tool was the next best thing to a weapon.

Meredith pulled up to the entrance, leaving a twenty-foot buffer zone between the truck and the door. From what she could see, the store was abandoned, deserted. The door was hanging ajar, but there was no movement from inside.

"Wait here," John instructed.

She watched as he climbed out of the vehicle, shovel in hand, and then clicked the door shut behind him. The hum of insects wafted through the broken windshield—a constant reminder of their lack of protection. She kept her foot on the gas and the vehicle in drive, ready to flee at a moment's notice.

John's boots crunched the pavement as he crept toward the store. When he reached the entrance, he used the shovel to open the door and peer inside. Meredith kept her eyes glued to the opening, but saw nothing but furniture inside. If any of the creatures were inside, they were hidden. John slipped through the door.

She waited in silence. The engine purred. Seconds later, he emerged and gave her the thumbs up.

"We're good. Can you pull around back?"

"What are we here for, John?" she called through the windshield.

"Supplies," he said simply, before heading back into the store.

She shrugged, then released her foot from the brake and rolled to the rear of the building. John was already on his way out of the store. In his hands was a large piece of wood. He brought it to the pickup's cab and dropped the door. She noticed he was wincing.

"Is your leg all right?"

"I'll manage. But I could use some help."

He grinned at her, and she smiled back. She switched the car into park and hopped out to join him, leaving the engine running. John slid the piece of wood—a four by eight—into the truck and walked back inside.

John motioned to a pile of wood he had stacked in one of the corners.

"Luckily I just stocked up the other day."

"What's all this for?"

"It *was* for the Daley's kitchen."

"And now?"

"Now it's what we're going to use to board up the windows of your house. If we have any chance at surviving this thing, we'll have to make sure no one gets inside."

"I knew I saved you for a reason."

"Never underestimate a woodworker."

25

"**I** DON'T LIKE THIS THING," QUINN said, peering out over the windowsill of the SUV. Dan watched as she stretched her seatbelt, straining to get a better view of the graffiti spray-painted on the hood. In spite of her comment, he could tell that she was feeling better. After their run-in with the men in fatigues, she'd been shaken up, terrified. Now she seemed a bit more at ease.

Although Dan missed the station wagon, Ken had been right—the SUV was more secure than what they'd been driving before. If nothing else, it was higher off the ground, leaving them less vulnerable to the creatures' attacks.

Dan's gaze flitted to the rearview mirror, taking stock of the items they'd packed. Before parting ways with Ken and Roberta, they'd split up the weapons and food, as well as several gas cans that they'd found in the back of the vehicle.

With a full tank and almost a direct route to Settler's Creek on I-40, Dan was hopeful they'd have plenty of supplies to last them, allowing him to concentrate on the journey itself.

Several hours ago, they'd already passed the border into New Mexico. They were making better progress than Dan had hoped.

After leaving Ken and Roberta, Dan had been lucky enough to encounter several patches of uninhibited highway, allowing him to travel at a higher rate of speed. Whenever obstacles sprung up in the highway, he switched back to the desert and engaged the four-wheel drive.

Quinn had been watching the road intently the entire time. Her gaze flitted between the landscape and the debris on the road.

"Do you remember this drive?" he asked her.

"I think so."

"The last time we made it you were about six years old."

"I remember singing along to the radio and counting the cars we passed with Mom. I don't really remember much else, though."

Dan smiled at the memory.

"I remember that you asked a lot of questions. You were always very curious. I remember you reading aloud all the road signs to make sure we understood them."

"Do you think things will ever go back to normal, Dad?"

"I hope so, honey. They may not be the same as before, but I'm sure they'll be good again. Just in a different way."

Quinn nodded and let her eyes drift back out the window. At the moment they were driving on the desert, but having passed by a few broken-down cars, Dan was getting ready to switch back to the highway.

Before he could make the switch, his daughter pointed past him.

"Dad, look!"

He followed her outstretched hand to the interstate. On the horizon were several figures crouched in the road. Unlike many of the corpses they'd seen on the way, these bodies were moving. Dan slowed the vehicle, instinctively preparing for the worst. He let one hand off the wheel and felt for the Glock 9mm on his lap.

Instead of driving back onto the highway, he kept to the desert, veering as close as possible to the edge without getting onto it. The figures grew more distinct as they approached; soon they were driving next to them.

There were two people on the road, and both were crawling on hands and knees, heads bent. On closer inspection, Dan saw that they weren't survivors, but two of the creatures. The things craned their necks at the approaching vehicle, but neither made any attempt to stand.

Convinced they were in no immediate danger, he slowed the vehicle to a halt to study them closer.

"I don't like this, Dad. Can we keep going?"

"I'm sorry, honey. I just want to get a closer look. Something about them seems…different."

The creature closest to the vehicle had once been a woman. Her long, stringy hair fell in front of her face, but he could see the whites of her eyes as they wandered from the SUV to the road.

Without warning, the woman-creature collapsed on the ground, convulsing.

"Are they dying?"

Dan paused.

"It certainly looks like it."

The creature next to her — once an older man with a pointed chin and white and gray stubble — threw a pale arm in their direction and then fell sideways to join his companion.

A few days prior, one of the agents they'd encountered had indicated that the virus was to last a few weeks. By the looks of it, things were coming to an end much sooner. The thought filled Dan with mixed emotions: on one hand he felt a wave of hope, on the other a hint of sadness for the victims.

He fixed his gaze on the two writhing creatures on the ground. Since collapsing, neither had regained their footing. Their cries filled the air — soft, high-pitched moans that wafted over the highway and into the desert beyond.

For a split second, he wondered if they could feel pain. He certainly hoped not.

"We better get moving," he said.

He let his foot off the brake and continued driving, eyes focused on the road ahead.

By the time they reached the Texas border, it was mid-afternoon. In the hours preceding, they'd seen several more creatures on the highway, all in the same condition. They'd seen no signs of any additional survivors.

For the most part, Dan had been able to keep to the breakdown lane, riding adjacent to the littered cars and motorcycles. Now, as they approached the New Mexico-Texas border, the lanes were clogged solid.

Dan brought the SUV to a halt and surveyed the scene. The interstate was a wall of cars. Were it not for the desert around them, Dan could have easily mistaken the highway for a city street in the middle of rush hour.

Vehicles were wedged and sandwiched in every direction, motorcycles and RV's all fighting for the same spot in the road. Beyond them was a silent blockade of military vehicles.

It was the first glimmer of government intervention he'd seen.

The sight of the camouflaged vehicles gave Dan a sudden chill, though he didn't know why. In the past, the greens and blacks would have represented a sense of order and stability. Now, they were a sordid reminder that the government had failed.

He let his gaze drift from one side of the highway to the other. In the middle of the road was a median; overhead was a bridge. In neither direction did he see an indication that someone was alive.

He threw the SUV into park.

"What are you doing, Dad?"

"It looks like nobody's home. But there's a possibility we can reach someone from one of the military vehicles."

"Do you think someone will be able to help us?"

"It's a possibility."

Dan looked back and forth between the road and daughter. The distance between the SUV and the military blockade was a few hundred feet. He expected her face to be lined with worry, but instead she met his eyes with resolve.

"Go, Dad. I'll be fine."

"Are you sure?"

She nodded. He handed her the 9mm from his lap.

"I'll keep you in my line of sight at all times. If you see something and I don't, honk the horn."

"Got it."

He smiled and patted her head, then dipped into the back seat for another weapon. Pistol in hand, he stepped out onto the open highway.

He shut the door and scoured the area.

In order to proceed, they'd need to drive off the road. The desert landscape was getting more and more difficult to navigate—a new crop of green shrubs and bushes had appeared at the road's edge. Although they hadn't had any issues yet, he hoped they didn't pop a tire.

He glared at the five military Humvees that were parked behind a row of barracks.

I wish we could take one of those.

But getting them out would be impossible. Each was flanked on all sides by pedestrian vehicles. There would be no way to get them free.

He let his gaze drift up and down the road. He could only imagine the panic that must have inspired the scene. All around him were bodies — both on the road and in the cars — and most were days old.

As he walked up the interstate, he came across a few bodies that looked like the infected.

Like the rest, these were lifeless and still, but these were fresh.

Is it over?

He shook his head at the scene and kept moving. After all they'd been through, it was hard to believe that it might come to an end. The last week had seemed like a never-ending battle, a war that held no victors.

He closed in on one of the Humvees. The door was ajar; a dead soldier in army gear was hanging out of the driver's seat. Dan worked his way to the passenger's side of the vehicle, then he opened the door and got inside. He rifled through the interior, finding a few rations and some papers. None of the paperwork made any sense.

He was reaching for the glove box when he heard a hissing noise that resembled static. It was coming from the dead solider in the driver's seat. He followed the noise until he found the source — a handheld radio by the man's feet.

He picked it up and held down the button.

"Hello? Is anyone there?"

He let go of the button, but the fuzz persisted. "Hello?"

He twisted several knobs and tried again, but there was no response.

Dammit.

He set the radio on the seat and wrenched open the glove box, but found nothing. Discouraged, he slid out of the vehicle. His boots had just hit the asphalt when he heard a voice answer him on the radio.

"Johnson?"

He leapt back into the vehicle and retrieved the radio, tapped the button. His heart was pounding.

"Hello? Can you hear me?"

"Yes, I hear you."

"This is Officer Dan Lowery from the St. Matthews Arizona police department. Whom am I speaking to?"

"This is Lt. Simmons from the United States Army at Fort Hood. Are you alone, Officer?"

Dan glanced at the inanimate figure next to him. The soldier's eyes were rolled back in his head, his mouth agape.

"I think so. I'm with my daughter, but it doesn't look like anyone else survived."

The radio was silent for a second. Dan repeated himself.

"Did you catch that?" he asked.

"I heard you, Officer."

"We're on I-40 at the border to Texas, on the New Mexico side. Can you send help?"

"I would if I could. But I'm the only one here."

"What do you mean?"

"Everyone else is dead, Officer Lowery."

The line returned to silence, and Dan felt his chest tighten. The hope he'd felt just seconds before dimmed.

"Are you OK?"

"I wish I could say I was, but I think I've been infected. And even if I wasn't, I'm surrounded on all sides. There's no way out of this room I'm in."

"Maybe I can help you, if you'll—"

"Believe me, Officer, if there was a way out of here, I'd know how to get to it. And in any case, it's too late for me."

"I'm sorry."

"It's not your fault."

"Lieutenant?"

"Yes, sir."

"How bad is this thing?"

"It's bad. As far as we know, the southwest is gone. We're working on preserving the borders to the surrounding states, but last I heard, it wasn't looking good."

"How about Oklahoma? Has it hit there yet? That's where we're headed."

"I think you might be out of luck, Officer. As far as I know, it's already crept over the state line. Even if you could get there safely, I wouldn't advise it."

Dan clutched the phone, his hand shaking. His entire plan—his last remaining hope—had just been shut down.

"What would you suggest we do?"

"I'd head north. Try to get ahead of this thing, if you can."

"Do you know if—"

"I'm sorry, Officer, but I need to go."

"But Lieutenant, I still have more—"

"If you don't mind, sir, I'd like to finish this letter I'm writing to my kids before it's too late. Best of luck, Officer."

Dan tried speaking several more times, but the man on the other end was gone. He stared out across the interstate at his daughter, over the wreckage that had become their lives, and did his best not to scream.

"What'd the man say, Daddy?"

"He didn't know much, honey. He's trying to get to someplace safe, like us."

"Are we going to meet up with him?"

"I don't think so. It'd be too far of a drive, and too dangerous."

Dan steered the vehicle off the road, weaving around a pair of bushes while his daughter peered through the windshield at the road ahead. Beside them, a green sign announced their arrival into Texas.

"Where are we going?"

"We're going to Oklahoma."

"We're still going to Aunt Meredith's, right?"

"Of course."

"How much longer do we have?"

"We're almost there. If we get moving, we should be able to make it before nightfall."

"Daddy?"

"Yes?"

"I can't wait to see her."

"Me, neither, sweetheart. Me neither."

26

EREDITH HELD THE BOARD TO the living room window while John tapped the nail.

"Is this the last one?" she asked.

"I think so. We should do another walk-thru to be sure."

In the past few hours, they'd systematically boarded up all the lower windows in the house. They'd started by using the wood in the furniture shop, then they'd taken loose pieces of wood they'd found in Meredith's barn.

When they were finished, Meredith sat on the edge of the couch to catch her breath. Her arms were sore from the lifting, cutting, and nailing, but it was a small price to pay for security.

Even with the windows boarded, she knew they wouldn't be safe enough.

Despite still being in danger, being at home and surrounded by familiar belongings had given her a sense of calm. In some way, it seemed like the events of the last day had been the product of her imagination, that she was still feeling the effects of a lingering nightmare.

Her property looked the same as it always did—rows of grass and corn in the backyard, a wire fence lining the roadside in the front. Past the driveway she could see the red barn that she'd recently repainted. There were no signs that anything unusual had occurred in the area, and no signs of the infected.

Still, she knew that things could change at any moment. And because of that, she needed to stay mentally prepared.

Meredith reached up and massaged her temples, fighting off a migraine headache. She was suddenly hit with a wave of exhaustion. She hadn't slept at all the night before, and it was catching up to her. As if sensing her mood, Ernie jumped onto her lap and started lapping at her face with his tongue. She smiled and gently pushed him down, then scratched him behind the ears.

It'd been good to reunite with him again. She felt guilty for even leaving him in the first place.

"I'm sorry I left you for so long, boy," she told him. "It won't happen again."

John paced the house, still favoring his injured leg. Since arriving home, she'd changed the bandage and cleaned it, but she could tell he was still in pain. She watched as he padded from one room to another, doing his best to put on a brave front. In spite of being in the house, she could tell he was still unsettled.

"You don't have any other guns in the house, do you, Meredith?"

"No," she replied. Having lost both of their

rifles during their journey, they were virtually defenseless.

"Maybe one of the neighbors has one."

"I don't think we should go back out there, John," she said. "We should probably just hang tight."

John glanced at the floor of the living room, where he'd collected a pile of makeshift weapons. In the stack were several garden tools, some knives, and some two-by-fours.

"If we get surrounded again—like I did at the furniture shop—we're going to be in trouble," he said.

Meredith sighed. They'd just reached the house a few hours ago, and already they were talking about leaving. The thought made her nervous and uncomfortable.

"I don't know, John. With your leg, I think you really need to rest."

"I'm feeling a lot better. You did a hell of a job stitching me back together."

He sat down beside her, placed his hand on her leg, and smiled.

"Flattery will get you everywhere," she said. She leaned over and kissed him on the lips, then wrinkled her nose. "You need a bath."

"Maybe I'll take one later."

"Who knows how long the power will last. You might as well take one while things are quiet."

"I'll take one when I get back."

"I can see where this conversation is headed.

No matter what I say, you're insisting on going out." She shook her head.

"Do you think the Sanders will have a rifle?"

Meredith thought for a minute. Aside from Sheila Guthright, Ben and Marcy were her closest neighbors. Although she couldn't swear that they had a rifle, it was possible they might.

"I think that would be the safest bet. Their house is only a few minutes away."

Resolved, John stood up and walked toward the door.

"I'll be back before you know it," he said.

"John, wait!"

Meredith stood and walked after him. Before he could leave, she grabbed him by the arm.

"There's no way I'm letting you go alone. I'm coming with you."

"Meredith—"

"No arguments, John. Let's get going."

After a quick debate, it was decided that John would drive the pickup. Although his left foot was injured, his right was unimpaired, and he insisted on giving Meredith a break.

Meredith watched closely out the passenger's-side window, purveying the endless fields, but saw nothing suspicious. Ernie sat on her lap, sucking in the air from the open window. Rather than leaving him behind, she'd decided to take him.

If something were to happen, she didn't want to leave him behind again.

Regardless, she could only hope that the journey was quick and safe. If all went well, they'd be home in half an hour. Maybe less.

They made the drive in silence. The air was thick with tension and uncertainty, but Meredith was glad to be next to John once again. When she looked over at him, she was filled with a sense of hope and completeness that she hadn't felt in a while. She just wished that she'd made the realization sooner, that circumstances were different.

The Sanders' home was about a half mile up the road; in no time the house was in view. The house, a white ranch with black shutters, sat several hundred feet from the road. Leading up to it was a driveway of crushed stone.

Unlike many of their neighbors, the Sanders didn't rely on their land for income. Ben worked from home as a computer developer, and Marcy taught second grade in the local elementary school. Because of that, the land was sprawling and mostly untouched. As far as she could tell, it was unoccupied.

John turned the pickup into the driveway. The crunch of stone seemed to shatter the quiet around them; Meredith envisioned a horde of creatures emerging from the horizon, awakened by the approaching vehicle, but none came.

Seconds later they'd pulled up next to the house.

John let the vehicle idle.

"Do you think the door's open?" he asked.

"I know where they keep the spare key." Meredith shifted in her seat. "I'll go inside."

"Nonsense."

"I know the layout of the house better than you do. It'll take me less time to search it."

"Skip it, Meredith. I'm coming with you."

John smiled, and she felt a surge of warmth. Meredith exited the vehicle. John did the same. The two of them followed a stone walkway to the front of the house, eyes fixed on the door and windows. Everything seemed locked and secured. Perhaps whatever happened to Ben and Marcy had occurred after they'd already left.

When they reached the front door, Meredith stooped off the front step and retrieved the spare key, which was hidden underneath a fake rock next to the landing. She inserted the key into the front door and waited.

There were no sounds from within. The area remained quiet save the idling of the pickup in the driveway behind them. She turned the key and pushed.

The door opened without a sound.

After a moment's hesitation, the two of them stepped through the threshold.

The interior of the house was far different from the exterior. From a distance, the house seemed peaceful, undisturbed. Inside, the home was in disarray. Lamps were knocked over, tables were overturned, and furniture was shifted. They had entered through the living room; past it was the kitchen. Meredith could see the open back door from here, which appeared to have been busted open.

It was as if the house had been ransacked.

In previous visits the house had been in perfect order, everything in place. Marcy had always kept an immaculate home. The scene was unsettling, to say the least.

"Come on," Meredith said, tugging John's arm.

Even though she knew the Sanders were dead, she still felt like an intruder.

She led John through the living room and into the dining room, then down a lone corridor beyond it. Although she wasn't positive where the rifle would be — she wasn't even sure they *had* one — she guessed that it would be in the bedroom.

The bedroom was cluttered and torn apart. Meredith let go of John's hand, and the two began their search. It didn't take more than a minute to find what they were looking for. In the corner of the room was a gun cabinet.

"Over here!"

The oak cabinet was long and rectangular, sporting a beveled glass front and a keyhole on the side. Inside the cabinet was an identical pair of .22 caliber rifles.

"His and hers." John gave a wry grin.

Meredith tried the door, but it was locked and wouldn't budge.

"Dammit. We need a key," she said.

She looked around the room, wondering where the key might be located. Was it on one of the Sanders' key chains? If so, it was possible that the keys might be in Ben or Marcy's pockets. If they couldn't find a key, they'd have to break the glass.

Aside from the gun cabinet, the room contained two bureaus, a bed, and a nightstand. Meredith moved toward the surrounding furniture and began opening drawers, starting with the closest bureau. She rifled through piles of underwear, socks, and t-shirts, but saw no sign of a key.

John ducked out into the hallway.

"I'll check the kitchen," he said. "If we don't find it, we'll break it open."

Meredith checked each drawer in turn, but with no luck. Having finished with the bureaus, she moved on to the nightstand. Inside the lone drawer was a pair of watches, a stack of jewelry, and two pairs of reading glasses.

Underneath was a key.

"I've got it!" she shouted.

From the other room, she heard John rummaging through kitchen drawers. It appeared he hadn't heard her. Undaunted, she brought the key over to the gun cabinet and slipped it into the lock. It fit perfectly. She turned, listened for the *click*, and then opened the door.

She removed each of the rifles from their perches and laid them on the bed. The weapons felt good in her hands. Inside the cabinet were also several boxes of shells, and she pulled them out and set them next to the guns.

It wasn't until she shut the cabinet that she realized the other room had gone quiet.

"John?"

The house was silent. She peered into the hall but saw no sign of him. Where had he gone? She picked up one of the rifles and walked toward the doorway, her breath accelerating with each step. If he'd been in trouble, surely she would have heard it.

Wouldn't she have?

The hallway was vacant. Down at the end, she could make out half of the kitchen and dining room, but saw no sign of the companion she'd arrived with. Rather than call out his name again, she treaded lightly, doing her best to deaden her footsteps on the floorboards.

What if he'd turned?

After all they'd been through, it was a possibility she'd never even considered. But now, walking through the silent household, she felt panic spreading like tendrils through her body.

Everyone else in town had already been infected. What if John was next? Hell, what if *she* was? There was no way to know. Right?

She crept forward, reaching the kitchen, and then stopped. The archway to the living room was on her left, and she glared into the room, hoping to find evidence of her missing companion.

When she finally caught sight of him, she breathed a sigh of relief. John was pressed against the far wall staring at her.

She advanced another step, but he held up his pointer finger to stop her. She followed his gaze to the other end of the kitchen and through the open back door.

Pacing back and forth in a small garden was one of the creatures.

The thing was wearing blue overalls and a baseball cap; Meredith recognized it as Paul Stevens, one of her distant neighbors. From what she could tell, Paul hadn't seen them.

Meredith kept to the edge of the kitchen, making her way along a refrigerator, cabinets, and a sink. Her hope was that she could reach the back door and close it. She clutched the rifle to her chest, hoping that she wouldn't have to use it.

When she reached the doorway, she peered outside. The creature had stopped next to a vine of tomatoes, sniffing the air. Meredith reached for the door handle. The hinges of the door swung outward. In order to reach it, she'd need to expose her arm outside, risking being seen. The creature was only twenty feet away.

She reached out and clasped her fingers around the handle. Before she could pull it, Paul Stevens turned and looked at her. She cried out in surprise and slammed the door. Seconds later he began pounding against it with his fists. She flipped the catch and engaged the deadbolt.

"I think that's our cue to leave," John said.

Meredith held up her weapon.

"The other rifle is in the bedroom. I found shells, too."

"Let's grab them and get the hell out of here."

The two of them flew for the bedroom, gathered the remaining gun and ammunition, and made for the front door. If they were lucky, the locked back door would keep Paul Stevens occupied for a while.

As they exited the house, Meredith could still see the back door rattling against the frame. She slammed the front door shut behind them, raced for the truck, and jumped inside.

Ernie began to bark, his nose in the air, and she did her best to calm him down. John switched into reverse and backed up in a U-turn, then roared down the driveway.

"That was a close call," John said, wiping a bead of sweat from his brow.

"I'm glad you saw him before he saw us."

She held the rifle between her legs and stared out the window. Although they'd escaped unharmed, the fact that Paul Stevens had made it to the Sanders' made her concerned. Where there was one thing roaming, there'd be others, and eventually they'd make their way to Meredith's house.

She just hoped that when the time came, they'd be able to ward them off. John looked over at her, seeming to read her thoughts.

"Do you still want to go back home?"

"Yes. If this is the end, John, there's no place I'd rather be."

He nodded and took her hand. Outside, the sights had returned to normal. Grass, fields, and sun abounded. She could already see her house on the horizon, and she tried to dispel thoughts that this would be the last time she'd see it from this angle.

A few seconds later, John pulled the pickup into her driveway.

Ernie had begun to pace on her lap, twisting in circles as if he were nervous.

"What's wrong, boy?"

She scratched his head, but he continued to act anxious. Soon after he stopped in place and barked.

"What's gotten into you?" she asked, patting his head.

When she followed the dog's stare, she saw what'd spooked him. Parked at the top of her driveway, covered in metal and graffiti, was a car she didn't recognize.

27

DAN SAT IN THE SUV and stared at the empty driveway. His heart sank. The windows of Meredith Tilly's house were boarded up; there was no sign of life from inside. He'd tried knocking on the doors several times, but to no avail.

It was possible she didn't even live here anymore.

How long has it been, Dan? Five years?

He shouldn't have let things go on this long. He should have patched things up years ago.

He thought back to the arguments that his wife and sister-in-law had had. In hindsight, everything seemed so insignificant. There was no reason that Quinn should have been kept from her aunt for so long, no excuse for him not picking up a phone. Even if Julie hadn't called her, he should've called her himself.

Unfortunately, letting things go had been easier than fighting for them.

He put his head down on the steering wheel and sighed. Out of the corner of his eye, he could see his daughter watching him. He knew that he had to be strong, but all he felt like doing was giving up.

"Dad?"

He felt a hand on his arm, and he clenched his eyes shut.

"Dad?"

He breathed a long sigh.

"What is it, honey?"

"Someone's coming up the driveway."

Dan snapped to attention. He jolted upright, removed his pistol, and turned his head. His daughter was right. Advancing toward them was a black pickup truck. He squinted but was unable to make out the details of its occupants through the sun's glare. From what he could tell, there were two people in the vehicle.

It looked like a man was driving.

"Who is it, Dad?"

"I'm not sure."

Dan had parked the SUV facing toward the house. In hindsight, he should've backed into reverse. He just hadn't expected to find the house empty.

In truth, he hadn't known what to expect.

The last few hours felt like a blur of highways and desert, and his body was stiff from constant driving and lack of sleep.

Now, as he stared at the approaching vehicle, he wondered what would happen next. Would they be forced to flee again? After days of fighting and days of struggle, would they be once again displaced?

The pickup truck rolled to a halt behind them.

Dan kept one hand on the gun, one on the wheel.

The door of the pickup opened, and the man inside aimed the barrel of a rifle at the back of the SUV. Dan tensed, ready to throw the vehicle in reverse. Before he could make a move, something dark and black leapt from the inside of the pickup and darted toward the SUV.

"Dad! It's Ernie!"

Before Dan could stop her, his daughter sprang from the car. The dog made a flying leap for her arms, and she caught him in mid-air, laughing as his pink tongue lapped at her face.

Dan opened the door himself, lowering his gun. A man and a woman had disembarked the pickup and were now in full view. On the driver's side was a tall, dark-haired man wearing a t-shirt and jeans.

On the passenger's side was Meredith Tilly.

It took Dan a second to recognize her. His sister-in-law's blonde hair was longer than he remembered, and her features had aged, though only slightly. In spite of her differences in appearance, she was by all accounts a beautiful woman, and she reminded him of Julie. He strode forward across the asphalt, heading in her direction.

Meredith met him halfway, tears already streaking her face. She dropped the rifle she was holding and embraced him, and he clenched her tight.

"Oh my God," she whispered into his ear. "Is it really you?"

Quinn had put down the dog, and it ran circles around their legs, doing its best to jump in between them. Meredith tilted her head back and looked at Quinn.

"Quinn! My God, you're so big!"

She stooped to her knees and opened her arms, and Dan watched his daughter run to meet her.

"Aunt Meredith!"

The two of them hugged for a solid minute, the dog working its way between them. Dan walked over to the man he didn't recognize and extended his hand.

"I'm Dan Lowery, Meredith's brother-in-law."

"John Parish," the other man said. "I'm Meredith's…"

"We're dating," Meredith interrupted, a smile on her face.

A second later her expression faded. She looked back at the SUV, trying to get a better view of the inside, and then turned to look at Dan.

"Julie…?" she whispered. Her eyes welled up.

Dan shook his head, his throat suddenly filled with a lump he couldn't swallow. His daughter had resumed playing with the dog, and he waited until she was out of earshot before he spoke.

"She turned, Meredith. I'm so sorry. There was nothing we could do."

Meredith lowered her head and clenched her eyes shut. Dan watched as she struggled to compose herself, her breathing coming in short gasps. Dan felt needles of emotion prick him from the inside, but he struggled to remain calm.

He had to be strong for his daughter.

A few seconds later Meredith cleared her throat and picked up the rifle, still leaning on John.

"Why don't you two come on inside? We can talk there." She pointed to the boarded up windows. "It's not exactly the Ritz-Carlton, but it's safer than standing out here."

Dan attempted a smile and called to his daughter. The four of them locked the vehicles and stepped inside, Ernie in tow.

"Can I go upstairs, Dad?"

"Yes, but be careful."

Dan watched as his daughter bounded up the stairs two at a time, eager to explore their new surroundings. Before they'd settled in, Meredith and John had searched the premises, double-checking that nothing had gotten inside.

The house was clear.

With Quinn on the upper level, the three adults each took a seat in the dining room. They had sprawled their weapons across the table, making a collage of guns and handles, and Dan had brought in his stockpile of food and drink. Every so often, John would stand and check out the windows, watching for signs of trouble.

Dan stared across the table at Meredith. Although she'd composed herself, he could see that her eyes were still moist.

"I don't know where to begin," he said.

"Me neither."

"Things have been so chaotic the past few days that it feels like we've been living this forever."

"I know the feeling."

Dan launched into his story, narrating the events of the past few days in detail. Meredith and John listened intently, heads propped in their hands. Every so often they stopped to ask questions. Having been outside the contamination zone—at least until recently—they had no knowledge of the agents, no insight into the cause of the virus. Dan briefed them as best he could. He concluded with the dying infected they'd seen on the road in New Mexico and Texas.

"I think its coming to an end, at least for the people who were first afflicted. But from what you guys have told me it sounds like it's just started here."

"Everything was fine until yesterday morning. We'd been checking up on each other each day—the neighbors and myself—and nobody had seen anything out of the ordinary."

Meredith recounted her own tale, briefing him on her battles with the neighbors, John's rescue, and the subsequent struggle to return home.

When she was finished, Dan pursed his lips.

"I think if we wait this thing out, we have a

fighting chance. We have everything we need here: food, water, and a place to hunker down. Not to mention that this place is pretty secluded. Even if those things were to show up, we'll have plenty of warning."

Meredith leaned across the table and took his hands.

"I'm so glad you came," she said.

Dan nodded. "Me too. If you hadn't been here, I'm not sure what we would've done."

"I can't believe how grown up Quinn has gotten. When I saw her last, she was about half the size that she is now. She reminds me so much of..."

Meredith's voice trailed off and she wiped at her face.

"She's been my rock through this whole thing. Without her, I'm not sure what I would've done."

Dan sighed and stood from the table. John was at the back window, peering through a crack between two boards. He gave one last stare and then rejoined his comrades.

"Can I get you something to drink, Dan?"

"As a matter of fact, I wouldn't mind something."

John retrieved a glass from a kitchen cabinet and began to fill it with one of the waters Dan had brought in.

Despite the fact that they were in an infected area, Dan felt more secure than he had in days. The house looked the same as he remembered it. The living room and dining room were still wallpapered with a country pattern, the walls adorned with pictures and knick-knacks. Although he hadn't been here in over five years, the place had barely changed.

He focused his attention on one of the pictures hanging on the wall—a family portrait of Julie, Meredith, and their parents. In the photograph, Julie appeared to be in elementary school—her hair was long and braided, her smile wide. Her arm was around her sister.

Meredith was right. Quinn *did* look like her mother. He'd always known it, but the longer he looked at the picture, the more he saw the resemblance.

In light of the situation, Dan was glad that they'd managed to make it to Settler's Creek. In some ways, it felt like they'd returned home.

Julie would have wanted it this way.

Meredith caught his attention and smiled. She followed his gaze to the picture.

"Julie was eight years old there, and I was six. Can you believe it? Look at my outfit."

In the photograph, Meredith was wearing a pair of overalls, a white t-shirt, and a straw hat—a fitting ensemble for a farmer's daughter. The two of them chuckled.

"You always knew what you wanted," John said, returning with the glass of water.

"I still do." Meredith smiled.

Dan took a sip of the beverage, letting it linger in his mouth before swallowing.

"I'm glad you kept this place," he said.

"You are?"

"Yes."

"Thanks, Dan. It means a lot to hear you say that."

The three sat in silence for a minute, taking in the peacefulness of the moment. From upstairs, Dan could hear the patter of dog and child feet on the hardwood, and he smiled at the sound.

A moment later, before they could get used to things, the peacefulness was interrupted.

"Dad! Come quick!"

Quinn's voice echoed down the stairs, a timbre of fear reflected in her words. Dan and the others bolted from their chairs. They raced up the steps, meeting the little girl at the top of the landing.

"Out the front window!" she said.

She took off running into Meredith's bedroom, weaving around the queen-sized bed and over to the window. Unlike the ones downstairs, this window hadn't been boarded up, and they had a clear view of the front lawn.

Dusk had settled over the countryside, casting a maroon glow over the tips of the grass. And on the horizon, just past the road, a horde of creatures advanced.

28

"**Q**UICK! TO THE CARS!" DAN yelled.

He grabbed his daughter's shoulders and led her to the doorway. Outside, he could hear the groans and undulations of the infected growing closer.

There wasn't much time.

He started to descend the stairs and then stopped. Meredith and John had remained in the room; neither had moved.

"Meredith! John! We have to go! Now!"

He stared at them with wide eyes, waiting for them to react. Quinn waved her hands, as well, but they stayed in place.

"I'm not going, Dan," Meredith said.

"Are you kidding me?"

She shook her head.

Dan opened his mouth to argue, but quickly closed it. He recognized the look on her face, the tone in her voice. It was the same resolve she'd had when deciding to keep the farm all those years ago. No matter what he said or did, he wouldn't be able to change her mind.

"I'm staying, too," John said. His tone was calm and insistent, and he held onto Meredith with a steady hand.

Dan alternated his gaze between them and the window, watching the creatures spill across the property. If he and his daughter left now, it was possible that they'd make it to the SUV in time. But he'd have to decide soon.

Quinn grabbed his arm. "Daddy, we can't leave Aunt Tilly. We need to stay. We can help!"

Dan leaned down and gripped his daughter's shoulders, looked her in the eye. He was surprised to see that she was calm and composed. Just a few minutes ago she'd been playing with the dog, mindful of the adults talking downstairs. Now it was as if a switch had been flipped and she was ready to do what it took to survive.

For the past week, they'd been running and hiding, moving from one place to the next. In all that time, they'd never settled down and never gotten secure. On top of that, they'd driven hours to get here, surviving threats in all directions, and had been fortunate enough to find Meredith alive.

There was no way they could leave her behind.

It was time to take a stand.

"We're staying with you."

He saw a flicker of emotion cross Meredith's eyes, and John gave her a squeeze.

"Let's get downstairs and get prepared. We need all hands on deck. Quinn, come with me," Dan said.

Meredith and John sprang into action, racing past them to get downstairs.

Dan glanced back out the window to assess the

situation. The creatures were spread across the lawn; in under a minute, they'd gained ground and overtaken the fence.

"Let's go!" he told Quinn.

The two of them raced to the lower level, where they could already hear the scrape and clatter of weapons being hefted.

Within seconds, the pounding of fists had erupted all around them. Windowpanes shattered, and hands and nails raked at the boards. The creatures had them surrounded.

"Never mind the guns. Barricade the door!" Dan yelled.

He signaled to John, and the two of them slid one of the living room couches in front of the door, which was already buckling from the weight of multiple bodies against it. Once it was in place, they each grabbed an end of a nearby loveseat and carried it over to the back door.

"Do you have any more wood? I don't think the furniture is going to be enough."

John shook his head. "We used everything we had."

On the floor was the pile of weapons that Meredith and John had gathered earlier — knives, garden tools, and hand tools.

"You two protect the downstairs. Quinn and I will go to the second level and see if we can pick some off through the window. If things get bad, yell."

John nodded. "Got it."

Dan watched as the two of them retrieved knives from the floor, then each of them grabbed a rifle from the dining room table. Meredith sprang for the nearest boarded window—where a set of fingers had wormed their way through the cracks—and began to thrust a kitchen knife through the opening. The creatures hissed and spit from the other side.

Dan hoisted a rifle of his own and handed a pistol to Quinn.

"Let's go!" he told her.

The two of them pounded up the stairs, rounding the hallway and back into the main bedroom. When Dan looked out, his mouth fell open. The creatures fell over each other in a swarm, each trying to get ahead of the pack. They groped the house with hungry hands, eyes focused on the house and the people within. He noticed a few trying to clamber up the side, but the smooth vinyl provided little assistance, and they slid back to the ground without finding purchase.

Dan unlatched the window lock and flung up the sash. Then he lifted the screen and poked the tip of the rifle outside. With limited ammunition, his best bet was to aim for the thickest pockets of their attackers. If he could pick off those closest to the house, perhaps he could incapacitate several with one shot.

It was hardly a solution, but it was the best he could come up with for now.

The bedroom was seated on the corner of the

house. When he looked down, he could see the boarded-up windows of the dining room, and when he looked diagonal he could see the front porch. A cluster of creatures hovered against the front door, limbs flailing.

"Stay back, Quinn!"

His daughter stood behind him and blocked her ears.

He fired off a shot, watching two heads explode and another thing collapse from a gunshot wound to the chest. The fallen creatures were quickly overtaken, the porch still a teeming mass of flesh.

Dan aimed carefully. Fired again. The shot hit home, sending another few creatures sprawling off the porch and onto the lawn.

The sound of wood cracking distracted him, and when he looked down, he saw that the things had broken one of the boards that covered the living room window. He trained the rifle at the culprits, squeezing off several more shots to stave them off.

Despite his accurate shooting, they were hopelessly outmatched. There were more creatures than bullets, and even if he used his shots sparingly, there'd be no way to kill them all.

"Dan!"

Shouting erupted from downstairs, and he reared back from the window. Meredith was calling for assistance. Quinn squeezed in next to him and pointed her pistol through the window.

"I've got it, Dad," she said.

He patted her on the back and rushed to the stairwell just as gunfire erupted from below. He took the stairs two at a time, his breath ragged.

Meredith and John clung to their rifles, taking turns firing through a broken-out window in the back of the dining room. Two boards had given way; the nails had been ripped out of the wall. One by one the creatures poked their heads through the hole.

"We need to board it back up!" Meredith shouted.

"On the floor!" John shouted to Dan.

Dan put down his rifle, scooped up a box and the tool, and walked toward the opening.

"Hold your fire!" he shouted. "I need help!"

With the last burst of gunfire, the window had been temporarily cleared. Dan grabbed hold of one of the loose boards and put it back in place. Meredith scooted over next to him and held it while he fumbled with the nails. A pair of grotesque hands pushed against the other side, and Meredith lost her hold.

"Dammit!" she cried.

Dan swung the hammer through the window frame, battering it against the creature's skull, and the thing toppled to the ground.

"Try again!"

Meredith resumed putting it in place; this time Dan was able to get ahold of a nail and begun pounding. The board continued to shake. Undaunted, he grabbed an additional nail and hammered it into the wood. With one board in place, he reached for the next, dodging a pair of mottled gray hands.

He swung the hammer through the opening again. This time he caught the creature with the claw-end, and the metal dug into the thing's scalp. He pulled upwards and pried it loose, spraying the room with a stream of fluid.

After another minute of struggle, Meredith and Dan had repositioned the second board and covered the window. Even still, others were beginning to give way; it was only a matter of time before one broke.

"This isn't going to work for long!" Dan yelled.

"How many of them are there?"

"Too many! We need a better plan!"

John had taken hold of the knife, and had returned to jabbing it through the cracks in between the boards. Dan swiveled around the house. In each of the gaps, indiscernible masses flitted back and forth. Occasionally he saw an eye, an ear, or a nose, but he was unable to tell one from the next.

Dan grabbed a knife and joined his companions, watching the scene with increasing dread. With the windows covered and the lights on, he felt like an animal in a cage, the subject of a failed science experiment. For the past week, he and his daughter had been able to cheat death, staying one step ahead of the carnage that followed them.

Now they'd painted themselves into a corner.

Or rather, *he'd* painted them into a corner.

We shouldn't have stayed here. We should've left.

Try as he might, Dan was unable to dispel the thought that he'd made a mistake. And this time, that mistake was going to cost them.

29

EREDITH CRINGED AS SHE THRUST the blade between the boards. Each time she stabbed, the knife made a sickening crunch, and every time she pulled it back, it contained a new smattering of fluid.

Just a week ago her greatest worry had been producing enough vegetables to haul to the local farm stand. Now she was engaged in a struggle for her life, sticking a kitchen knife into the townspeople's flesh. The thought made her sick to her stomach.

At the same time, there were no other options.

It was Meredith's own hubris that made her stay, and now she'd put others in danger as well. She should've agreed to leave the farm. She shouldn't have stayed. A house could be replaced, but there'd be no replacing the ones she loved.

I'm sorry, she thought.

Rather than speak, she continued to stab through the window, thrusting and plunging while the others next to her did the same. If she let up for one minute, the creatures would prevail, and she wasn't about to let that happen. Not willingly, at least.

Not while I have any fight left in me.

A gunshot rang out from upstairs, and she jumped at the sound. Dan fled his post at the window.

"I'll be back!" he yelled.

She watched him disappear upstairs, saying a silent prayer that Quinn was all right. In spite of all the little girl had been through — in spite of losing her mother — she possessed a resilience that Meredith couldn't believe. She could already tell that Quinn would grow up into an amazing woman.

She just hoped they'd all be there to see it.

I have to figure a way out of this. There must be a way to get rid of these things.

Although it was possible they'd lose interest, she wasn't banking on it. The more likely scenario was that they'd get in the house first. Sooner or later they'd break through the doors and windows.

There had to be a way to distract them somehow, to lure them away.

Think, Meredith, think.

She wracked her brain, searching for an answer. Behind her, Ernie's nails clicked the hardwood as he paced the house, running from window to window. His bark filled the house. Meredith turned to check on him, then returned her gaze to the window.

There was no way they could shoot all the creatures, not with their limited ammunition. But what if they could lead them away and contain them?

A thought struck her.

"Dan!" she shouted.

She heard several more gunshots from upstairs. The noise echoed through the house. Afterward, the voice of her brother-in-law wafted down the staircase.

"We're all right!" he said. "Just holding them back!"

She looked next to her at John, who was thrusting his knife through the adjacent window. He met her eyes, perhaps sensing she had an idea.

"What is it?" he asked.

"We need to lure these things away from the house."

"How are we going to do that? We can't even get outside."

"If one of us can get out, maybe we can lead them to the barn. Maybe we can trap them inside."

"I love you, Meredith, but that's the craziest idea I've ever heard."

She dropped her knife to the floor and bridged the gap between them, grabbing hold of the fabric of his shirt.

"If we don't do something, we're going to die in here."

"Leaving now would be suicide."

The boarded windows in front of them shook and rattled.

"And staying here isn't?"

John stared at her, his face hardening with resolve. "I'll go," he said.

"No offense, but with your wounded leg you wouldn't last a second. And I know this property like the back of my hand. If anybody stands a chance out there, it's me. If I can lure them away, you, Dan, and Quinn can get to the SUV."

John opened his mouth to speak, but she silenced him. The groans of the creatures increased in volume, as if they were preparing to step through the walls themselves. She kissed him on the lips.

"I'll be back."

Without giving him a chance to respond, she darted from the dining room and up the stairs. John was right—the odds were stacked against her. Regardless, she owed it to her companions to try.

"I don't like this idea one bit," Dan said, shaking his head. "You can't go out there. Not now."

Meredith looked out the window of the second bedroom. Beyond it was a sloped roof about ten feet across that formed an overhang over the front porch. In the driveway were the two cars.

"I can get to the truck, Dan. All I need is a distraction."

"There are too many of them. Even if we could draw them away, they'd be back in seconds. It's just too risky."

Meredith furrowed her brow. Below them,

several of the creatures leapt up and slid down the vinyl siding. The overhang was about fifteen feet from the ground, just out of reach from their groping fingers. Dan clutched his pistol.

"How much ammunition do we have left?"

"I'm not sure, but it can't be much. Listen, Meredith, I wouldn't feel right letting you go out there."

She handed him the rifle she held in her hands.

"You're the best shot we have. We need you in here to hold them back."

He shook his head while she continued.

"It's my fault that everybody's chosen to stay here, Dan. If we'd left sooner, we could've gotten away. Now we're all trapped. Let me make this right. I can get us out of this. You just have to trust me." She grabbed his shoulders and looked him in the eye.

After a long hesitation, he nodded.

"Please be careful, Meredith. And don't take any chances. If things get bad, just keep driving."

"I will. I promise."

Meredith lifted her leg over the windowsill and climbed onto the roof. She patted the top of her pants, verifying she still had a pistol, and then tapped her pockets for the keys. The creatures stared up at her, eyes glossed and hollow. She looked back at the window, taking in the worried forms of her brother-in-law and niece.

"Are you ready?" Dan asked.

"Go," she mouthed.

She heard Dan and Quinn flee from the windowsill, then footsteps padding down the stairwell. Moments later she heard all three of her companions screaming and shouting from somewhere in the back of the house to create a distraction. She flattened herself against the vinyl siding.

The creatures below her changed direction, moving in tandem like a frightened herd. Were it not for their incessant moans and salivating mouths, it might have seemed like they were wounded prey fleeing an unseen predator, scared for their lives.

The yelling and banging continued. Meredith watched them leave, her heart pounding as she contemplated what she was about to do.

The ground was fifteen feet below her. If she were to twist or sprain something, that would be the end. Once she was on the ground, she'd be fair game for all of them. Even one would be enough to incapacitate her.

She clenched her eyes shut and thought of her sister.

You can do this, Meredith. You have no other choice.

Then, before she could have second thoughts, she crept to the edge and leapt off.

Meredith was only in the air for a second, but the sensation of falling seemed to last much longer. Before she could cry out, the ground sprung to meet her, and Meredith did her best to roll and absorb the impact. Her shoulder throbbed, but she was otherwise intact, and she was quickly able to roll sideways and away from the house.

When she came to a stop, she got to her feet and assessed her surroundings.

She'd made it to the ground in one piece.

Although the majority of the creatures had relocated, a few lingered, and they scrambled in her direction at the sight of her. Meredith withdrew her pistol and fired two rounds, striking the first in the head, the second in the arm. Without further hesitation, she broke into a run toward the pickup.

The shrieks of the creatures were even louder outside, and each one pierced her heart with a needle of fear. Within seconds, heavy footfalls thundered against the grass behind her.

She kept her eyes focused on the vehicle in front of her, knowing that she couldn't afford to look back.

To stop moving was to die.

When she reached the truck, she fumbled with the key, trying to fit it into the lock.

Come on!

The noise from her pursuers grew louder. She found the opening and turned the key, listening to the door unlock. Then she grabbed the handle, wrenched it open, and jumped inside. No sooner had she shut the door than bodies slammed into the exterior. When she looked to the left, she saw three vacant faces staring through the window.

She locked the doors and started the vehicle.

The engine purred underneath her, and she found herself filled with a new fear. What if the vehicle died?

Don't think about that now, Meredith.

She threw the vehicle into drive and hit the gas, propelling the vehicle forward. The tires found purchase on something — either on asphalt or on limbs — and the vehicle roared up the driveway, slowly veering toward the grass.

She eyed the moving masses in the rearview. Even with the speed of the vehicle, she wouldn't gain much ground on the creatures. As soon as the pickup stopped moving, they'd narrow the gap.

This isn't going to work, she thought frantically.

But it was too late. She'd already come this far. She had to try.

When she cleared the house, she saw where the bulk of the things were located — the majority of them were in the backyard. From inside, it'd been impossible to gauge how many of them there were. Now, she had a clear view of their situation. There had to be at least fifty of them. Things were looking grim.

The creatures pounded their fists at the boarded-up windows, their faces gnarled and gruesome. It looked like several pieces of wood had caved. She stopped the vehicle about twenty feet from the barn and honked the horn, keeping her eyes on the house. A few of the creatures began to follow the noise, but most remained in place.

She needed to lure them away from the property, to the fields behind it.

"Come on!" she screamed.

She rolled down the window and stuck her head out. In the driver's side mirror, she could see the things behind her getting closer.

"Over here, you pieces of shit!"

She waved her left arm out the window, pounding the horn with her fist. The creatures moaned louder, and one by one they fled the house and moved toward her. At this point she'd gained the attention of almost all of them. Once she'd led them far enough away, Dan, Quinn, and John could escape out the front.

Here they come. Be ready.

She glanced in front of her. The barn door was shut. She shook her head at her earlier idea. There would have been no way to corral the things inside.

She revved the gas, keeping one foot on the brake, watching the cluster of creatures grow closer. At this point they were almost on top of her. She eyed the fields off to her right. If she waited any longer, they'd be clawing at the pickup.

She was just about to take her foot off the brake when she heard an ear-piercing scream from the house. She turned her head just in time to see one of the boarded windows cave. Through the opening, she saw that Dan, Quinn, and John were still inside. Not one of them had escaped.

Behind her, a stream of creatures turned back for the house.

No! Wrong way!

Despite her efforts, Meredith had failed. The things swarmed the rear windows; a few wandered back to the front. The remaining creatures were closing in on the pickup, preparing to lunge. She had to move. She had to keep going. Dan's words echoed in her head.

"If things get bad, just keep driving."

But she couldn't do that. She couldn't leave them behind.

I need to do something. I can't let them die in there.

She glanced back at the barn. There had to be something she could use inside, something to deter them. Out of nowhere, an idea struck her.

It was a long shot. Probably even more so than what she had just attempted. But they were running out of time, and it was all she had.

She had to act.

Meredith let her foot off the brake and barreled forward, crashing against the doors and caving them inward. She drove ten feet into the barn and ground to a halt. Then she threw open the door and leapt out, the engine still running.

Her pursuers were gaining ground. She could hear their feet plodding against the grass. The barn was dark and shadowed, but there was no time to turn on the lights. She moved forward by memory, skirting around an ensemble of lawn equipment and hay, and felt for the two things she'd come to find. Her hands finally graced the side of one of the objects. She grabbed the two five-gallon metal canisters and hefted them back to the car, then jumped inside.

The creatures had reached the barn entrance, and they crashed through the doors, as if sensing that their window of opportunity was closing. She heard hands on the back of the pickup, but before the things could progress any further, she slammed the car into reverse, knocking them backward. The vehicle rose and the tires crushed something beneath the tread.

Suddenly she was out in the open again. Dusk was closing in, and so was the horde.

Thank God she'd gotten to the propane. She just hoped Dan was as good of a shot as he claimed.

The back of the house was flooded with creatures. Meredith drove a few hundred feet from the barn, honking the horn, keeping an eye on the window where she'd seen her companions. In the rearview mirror, she saw a flood of the things chasing behind her.

This isn't going to work. There's no way.

She ignored her inner voice filled with fear and doubt, and concentrated on leaving a buffer zone around the house. Even if she couldn't get rid of all of the creatures, maybe they could get rid of enough to escape. When she'd reached a distance of several hundred feet, she stopped the vehicle and grabbed the propane. Then she jumped out of the truck and placed the canisters on the ground.

Dammit. She needed a lighter.

She dove back into the truck and tore through the glove box, remembering there used to be one in there. *Come on.* Where was it? She remembered seeing one—an old red one that her father used to use. She'd left it in the glove compartment, thinking it might come in handy some time.

And now that time had come.

She pushed aside several bundles of paperwork, finding nothing, and then suddenly it was in her hand. She grabbed hold of it and leapt back outside, fumbling with the canisters.

She opened each of the nozzles. When the gas was flowing, she flicked the lighter, lighting each one and watching the flame take hold. Once they were lit, she hopped back in the truck and looked back at the house.

The first-floor windows were empty. No sign of Dan. Where was he?

She watched as several of the creatures wormed their way through the open window where she'd seen her companions before.

Dammit!

A mound of creatures raced toward her. She scanned the upper windows, hoping for a glimpse of her brother-in-law, but there was none to be found. Chances were that he was preoccupied, battling the creatures that were trying to break in. If that were the case she was out of luck. Too late.

The creatures advanced, snarling and moaning. In seconds she'd be overtaken.

She let her foot off the brake, ready to move, ready to let the plan go.

And then a face appeared in the upper bedroom window. She saw a hand — Dan waving to her, motioning for her to move — and she hit the accelerator. He'd seen her. He knew what she was trying to do.

The pickup raced forward, and she hit the gas, knowing she had to gain as much distance as possible. Within seconds she'd traveled to the driveway. She kept her eyes glued to the rearview mirror, waiting for the explosion to follow.

She heard a gunshot. Then two.

At first there was nothing. The creatures that had been pursuing her — about fifty or so, from the looks of it — started to disperse. A pit formed in her stomach, and she fought to suppress it.

And then she heard it — an explosion that rocked the air.

She glanced into the rearview mirror. The lawn behind her had become a ball of flame, casting orange and yellow ripples across the property. She hit the brake and ducked down in her seat, unsure of how far the shrapnel would travel, fearing that the vehicle would be hit. From behind her, the creatures shrieked and groaned.

She remained low, hands shaking, unsure of what to expect.

Would it be enough to incapacitate the bulk of the creatures?

When the noise had subsided, she raised her

head and peered behind her at the tattered lawn. The creatures had been decimated. Pieces of them were scattered across the grass; of those that remained, most were on fire. She watched them stagger sideways across the grass, their features melting under the lick of yellow flame.

A voice cried out in the distance, and she struggled to make out the words. She strained her ears, and suddenly the message became clear. It was Dan; he was shouting at her from the house.

"Swing the truck back around!"

Although she could barely hear him, she complied, yanking the wheel and driving back toward the explosion site. When she reached the vicinity, she kept to the perimeter of the yard — far enough away to avoid the burning creatures. Every few seconds the rifle clapped, and she watched the remaining creatures drop to the ground one by one, reduced to a mangled pile of skin.

When she reached the house, she pulled up to the broken rear window. Several creatures still milled about, and she fired off the remaining rounds of her pistol to hold them off.

Where were the others?

She stared through the opening, waiting for her companions to appear, but there was no sign of them. She glanced back into the yard. Though they'd incapacitated the majority of the creatures, they hadn't killed them all. Several of the things were unscathed, and when they took notice of Meredith in the pickup, they ambled toward her.

"Come on!" she shouted through the window.

A few seconds later she saw movement, and suddenly her companions were spilling from inside.

"Let's go!" she shouted.

Dan and Quinn appeared first, John limping behind them. One of the roaming creatures tried to snag Quinn, but Dan fired off a shot, knocking it to the ground. The air was thick with smoke and flame, and the three of them coughed from the smell.

A second later they were throwing the doors open and jumping inside, filling the vehicle with smoke and sweat. Meredith hit the gas.

The pickup sprang to life, propelling them across the lawn and onto the driveway. Behind them, a cluster of fiery bodies danced across the lawn, knocking against one another like broken marionettes. Meredith blinked hard and forced herself to look away.

Once they were out of immediate danger, she glanced at the seat next to her.

Quinn sat in the passenger's seat, her head buried in her lap. Meredith reached over and caressed the girl's hair.

"It's OK, sweetie," she said with a smile. "We made it."

30

"ARE YOU SURE YOU'RE OK with this, Meredith?" John asked. His face was lined with worry.

Meredith leaned on her shovel. Below her was the charred body of Paul Stevens, her old neighbor—the creature she'd seen at Ben and Marcy Sanders house. He must have traveled to the farm at some point during the attack.

"I'll be fine," she said.

It had been over a day since they'd left the farm. Meredith surveyed the backyard, which was still covered in bodies.

They'd been picking up remains for hours: hefting them into tarps, dragging them to the pickup, driving them to a remote corner of the lot. Meredith had insisted that they give the townsfolk a proper burial.

No one had argued.

In order to spare Quinn from the gory scene, Dan and his daughter had remained at the Sanders' house. Inside they'd found an assortment of blocks, puzzles, and dolls. After arriving, Meredith had recalled that the Sanders had had a niece; they'd probably kept the toys there for when she visited.

In any case, they'd been a welcome distraction for both Dan and his daughter.

Meredith stuck her shovel into the blackened lawn and wiped a bead of sweat from her forehead. She looked over at John, who still held a look of concern.

"Do you think it's over?"

"I hope we've seen the worst of it," John said.

She let her gaze drift to the house. Although the downstairs windows were boarded up, a few lights blazed upstairs. After all that had happened, it was a miracle the power was still on. She wondered how long it would last. With no one to maintain the power plant, it was possible that it would be cut off soon, but she was grateful for every moment they had it on.

"Are you sure you want to stay in town?"

"I've never been more sure of anything in my life," she said. "I'm through running. From my family, from the infection, from you..."

She let her shovel fall to the dirt and walked over to John, and the two locked lips under the inviting rays of the sun.

"Thank you, Meredith."

"For what?"

"For giving me a second chance."

"I wish this place had more bedrooms," Meredith

T.W. Piperbrook

said, fluffing the pillows and sheets she'd set on the floor of the Sanders' bedroom.

"Are you kidding me?" Dan laughed. "This is the best setup we've had in days."

She had set up Dan and Quinn in the second bedroom; she and John would sleep in the master. For the remainder of the night, they'd agreed to take shifts watching over the property. Since leaving Meredith's farm, there'd been no other signs of danger, but none of them wanted to take any chances.

It was a small price to pay for stability.

Meredith had agreed to take the first shift. Although she was tired, she knew that Dan and Quinn must be exhausted. They'd been on the run for days; they deserved to get some rest.

"Are you comfortable, Quinn?"

The little girl smiled at her from the bed through half-closed eyes. They'd been talking a few minutes, and already her niece was starting to relax. Meredith leaned over and kissed her on the head.

"I'm so glad you came to find me."

"Me too, Aunt Meredith."

Dan had arranged himself on the floor next to the bed. Meredith noticed he'd chosen a spot by the window. Even though it wasn't his turn to watch, she was sure he'd been keeping an eye out just the same.

The thought gave her comfort, and she smiled down at him in appreciation.

"Try to get some sleep," she told them.

"We will," Quinn said.

"Goodnight."

Meredith walked out of the bedroom, snapping the light off behind her.

When she went downstairs, John was in the kitchen, rifle propped at his side.

"Do you see anything?" she asked him.

"No. We're all clear for now. Why don't you head into the bedroom and get some sleep?"

"No, you go ahead and rest, John. I'll wake you up in a few hours when I get tired."

"You sure?"

"Positive."

He handed her the rifle. In the wake of the attack, they had only a few guns left with ammunition. Those they had left were stacked on the dining room table, easily accessible to anyone keeping watch. Since arriving, they'd cleaned up the house; Meredith had even transported some of her pictures and belongings from the farm. Between the fumes of the propane and the smell of the bodies, they'd decided to vacate her old house, at least for now.

John kissed her on the cheek and headed upstairs. She looked after him, then switched her focus to the boarded windows. Through the course of her shift, she'd make the rounds to all of them, keeping a careful watch on the premises.

Hopefully that would allow her comrades to sleep.

The wind gusted from outside, blowing a gentle breeze through the cracks and crevices. It was still summertime, and the fresh air felt refreshing against her skin. In the coming days they'd have to figure things out. They'd need to reinforce the windows, get more weapons, figure out a long-term plan.

But for now, she was just grateful that they'd all found each other, and that they'd all survived another day. In the wake of what had happened, there wasn't much more she could ask for.

Something brushed past her leg, and she jumped before realizing it was Ernie. He launched into the air, aiming for her arms, and she smiled. She picked him up and held him close.

The dog lapped at her face. Since arriving at the Sanders', he'd spent most of his time pacing, doing his best to get adjusted. Now it seemed like he was settling down.

"You know what, Ernie? We're going to get through this," she whispered. "And no matter what happens, we're all going to be OK."

31

F OR THE FIRST TIME IN days, Dan awoke not to the sounds of a disturbance, but to the smell of a home-cooked meal. He rolled over in his sheets and rubbed at his eyes. Even though he'd lain down, he hadn't expected to sleep.

He glanced up at the bed next to him. The sheets were rumpled; his daughter was gone. For a split second he felt a tinge of worry, then he heard the sounds of laughter from the other room.

It was a sound he hadn't heard in a while, and it felt damn good to hear it again.

He rose to his feet and looked out the window, which he'd kept open. The sun shone through the windowpane, promising another day of light and warmth, and a few birds circled overhead. He ignored the memories in his head and did his best to focus on the smells coming from the kitchen.

Still fully dressed, he turned and walked across the room, then padded down the stairwell. The dining room table was set. Meredith and Quinn sat across from each other, and John sat at the window with a plate on his lap.

"Am I the last one up?" Dan asked.

The rest of them smiled.

"You almost missed lunch, Dad!" Quinn said.

Meredith pointed to a place setting at the head of the table, where a plate full of garden-fresh potatoes and vegetables awaited. Dan pulled out the chair and sat, feeling more grateful than he had in days. He took a bite of his potatoes. Even though they were a little cold, he found himself thinking they were the best he'd tasted.

Sometimes a meal was only as good as the company you kept, and right now, he couldn't have asked for better companions.

"How are things looking outside, John?"

"All clear since last night."

"That's great news."

Dan took another forkful of food and wiped his chin with a napkin. He studied the man perched at the window. In all the commotion of the night before, he'd hardly gotten the chance to know him.

"So what did you used to do, John? I mean, before all this…"

"I was a woodworker. I have a furniture shop in town. That's how Meredith and I met, actually."

Meredith pointed to the boarded windows, which they'd transported from the farm. "All this wood was from his store."

"You seem like a good guy to have around."

The four shared a laugh. Quinn speared a piece of tomato with her fork, dropping it onto the floor on the way to her mouth. Ernie swooped in to pick it up.

"Ernie!" Meredith scolded. "Mind your manners."

The dog licked Quinn's pant leg in apology. She patted him on the head, leaning down to give him a kiss of her own.

"It's OK, Ernie. I would've shared it with you anyway."

When everyone had finished eating, Meredith stood from the table and reached for the empty plates.

"Anyone for seconds?"

Dan paused for a moment. His stomach was still rumbling; it'd been a while since they'd had a decent meal.

"Sure," he said.

Meredith retrieved the dishes and returned to the counter.

"How long do you want to stay here?" she asked.

Dan paused, glancing around the room at his companions. For the first time in over a week, he had no pressing desire to leave. In just over a day, the Sanders' had become not only a place of shelter, but also a place of familiarity; a place that felt like home.

"I'll have to check our appointment book. We don't have anywhere to be, do we Quinn?"

The little girl shook her head and smiled.

"Well, I have enough food to last for a while," Meredith said. "Between the crops I brought from the farm and the packages you brought from the car, we should be all set for a while."

"That's great news."

"I also saw a nice garden out back. I'll bet we can harvest the crops."

"Excellent," Dan said.

"There's a catch," she said, holding up her finger.

"What is it?"

"I'll need help. Anyone who wants to eat is going to have to work for it." Meredith grinned.

Quinn immediately raised her hand. "I'll help you, Aunt Meredith!"

"Anything for a meal!" Dan quipped.

The group laughed. John rose from his perch.

"You don't have to worry; Meredith is a great teacher. Before helping her on the farm, I couldn't even look at a plant without killing it."

"Now he's a regular farmhand," Meredith said, punching his arm.

"We'll need to figure out schedules for keeping watch, too. Maybe take some trips into town for more supplies."

"Let's talk about that later," Dan said, giving the others a warm smile. "For now, let's just enjoy our meal."

The others nodded and turned to other conversation.

Within minutes, laughter filled the room. In the coming days, they'd have a lot of things to figure out. But all that could wait. Regardless of what had transpired, regardless of what the world had become, they'd found each other.

And right now, that was the only thing that mattered.

REVIEWS

If you enjoyed CONTAMINATION 4: ESCAPE, PLEASE leave a review, as this would be a HUGE help in allowing others to discover my works and will allow me to keep doing what I love most: writing!

Take care and happy reading!

-Tyler

Want to know when the next book is coming out?
Sign up for NEW RELEASE ALERTS
and get a FREE STORY!
http://eepurl.com/qy_SH

ABOUT THE AUTHOR

T.W. Piperbrook was born and raised in Connecticut, where he can still be found today. He is the author of the **CONTAMINATION** series, the **OUTAGE** series, and the co-author of **THE LAST SURVIVORS**.

He lives with his wife, a son, and the spirit of his Boston Terrier, Ricky.

LIKE him on Facebook at: www. facebook.com/twpiperbrook

READ ON FOR A PREVIEW OF
CONTAMINATION 5: SURVIVAL

BOOK 5: SURVIVAL

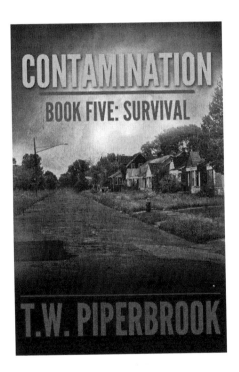

PART ONE
HUNTED

"OVER HERE!"

The men were coming. Through the haze, Noah could hear the rumble of motors and the cry of voices. He struggled to open his eyes, but they were swollen shut. His face burned with pain.

After a few attempts, he cracked his eyelids. The rays of the midday sun pierced his retinas, and he squinted to reduce the glare. The fact that he was alive was either a miracle or a curse; at the moment, he couldn't decide which. He wiggled his fingers and toes. As far as he could tell, nothing was broken.

But that didn't make him feel any better.

He lifted his head, biting back a fresh swell of pain. He was lying in the forest, about fifty feet from the road. Around him was a legion of pines. Just minutes ago, he'd been thrashing through the underbrush, hoping to find respite in the depths of the forest. After expending his last bit of energy, he'd dropped to the ground behind one of the large, sap-covered trunks.

Now he lay exhausted, listening to his pursuers approach.

He patted his pockets, hoping to find something

he'd missed, but his ripped khaki shorts were empty. His only hope was to summon enough strength to continue.

If he didn't move, he'd die.

He thought of his family in Portland and clenched his teeth. For the past few days, the image of Mom, Dad, and Ricky had been the only thing keeping him going. Now he found himself wondering if he'd ever see them again.

Don't give up now.

Noah forced himself to his knees, ignoring his aching muscles, and crawled through the thickets. *Keep low, and keep moving.* He needed to put distance between himself and the road. If the men couldn't find him, perhaps they'd grow bored and stop looking so closely; maybe they'd even give up.

The forest floor crackled under the weight of men's footsteps. The men had stopped talking, but their breathing echoed through the trees behind him. In a matter of minutes, Noah had become their target, their prey. Seconds after seeing him, they'd forced his truck off the road and into a tree.

If only he'd taken another road...

For the past few days, he'd been practicing the art of avoidance, doing his best to steer clear of the infected and the survivors. After a few close calls with trigger-happy lunatics, he'd been hesitant to trust anyone. At the same time, he'd known the solitude couldn't last forever. Sooner or later he'd be forced to fight or flee. As much as he hated to admit it, his current situation was long overdue.

He should've stayed at the salvage yard in Arizona.

Leaving his former companions behind had been one of the hardest things he'd had to do, and the guilt had eaten at him for days. He could only pray that Sam, Delta, Dan, and Quinn were safe.

But he needed to find his family. Whether they were alive or dead, he needed to find them. He needed to *know.*

He scrambled ahead through the forest, listening to the snap of underbrush behind him, using his pursuers' movements as cover. When they moved, he moved. When they stopped, he stopped. He darted from tree to tree, using the thick trunks for cover as if he were in the real-life version of a video game.

His vision was still bleary from losing his glasses. His prescription was weak, but he'd been wearing them regularly for driving, and his eyes struggled to adjust.

Beads of sweat dotted his forehead. Over the course of the day, the sun had grown progressively hotter, and as he ran, it enveloped him like a warm blanket. Aside from his tattered shorts, Noah was wearing only a polo shirt and shoes. He should've been comfortable, but instead, he was red and overheated.

One of the men coughed.

Noah ducked behind a tree. After a few

seconds, he peered behind him. On the road, a few hundred feet away, he could see his pickup truck. All four tires had been flattened; the hood was smoking. One of the men was standing guard next to it.

His pursuers weren't letting him get away. If he doubled back, he'd be trapped. His only hope was to head deeper into the woods.

Hide or move.

Noah clambered forward. Given that the men had rifles, he was hopelessly outmatched. There was no way he could face them.

One glimpse of him and they'd shoot.

He continued on. After several more minutes of running, he realized the men had stopped. He listened closely as their low, muffled voices seeped through the forest. What were they talking about? What were they planning?

Noah assessed his situation. The forest in front of him was thick with foliage, but there was a clearing in the distance.

If he could get to it, perhaps he'd find help.

The area he was in wasn't exactly brimming with people, but civilization had to exist somewhere. He stared at the distant patch of light, gauging how many steps it would take him to get there.

Twenty? Twenty-five? How far could he go before he was shot down?

Staying where he was would mean certain death. He'd rather die on his feet than be mowed down on his knees.

Behind him, the forest fell into silence.

He flexed his hands and prepared himself to run.

This is it, Noah. This is your last chance at escape.

Gritting his teeth, he broke from the trees and ran.

Want to read more?
CONTAMINATION 5: SURVIVAL
is Available Now!

COMPLETE CONTAMINATION SERIES AVAILABLE NOW!

CONTAMINATION PREQUEL
CONTAMINATION 1: THE ONSET
CONTAMINATION 2: CROSSROADS
CONTAMINATION 3: WASTELAND
CONTAMINATION 4: ESCAPE
CONTAMINATION 5: SURVIVAL
CONTAMINATION 6: SANCTUARY

OTHER SERIES:

OUTAGE 1
OUTAGE 2: THE AWAKENING
THE LAST SURVIVORS (co-
written w/Bobby Adair)

Contamination 4: Escape
Copyright © 2013 by T. W. Piperbrook. All rights reserved.

First Print Edition: June 2015

Proofreading by Red Adept.
Cover Design: Keri Knutson
Print Formatting by Streetlight Graphics
Special thanks to Nicholas Spragg.

For more information on the author's work, visit:
http://twpiperbrook.blogspot.com/

Dedicated to my son Liam, for providing me with endless inspiration and joy.

49247838R00184

Made in the USA
San Bernardino, CA
18 May 2017